Albert B. Weymouth

A Memorial Sketch of Lieut. Edgar M. Newcomb

of the Nineteenth Mass. Vols

Albert B. Weymouth

A Memorial Sketch of Lieut. Edgar M. Newcomb
of the Nineteenth Mass. Vols

ISBN/EAN: 9783337885113

Printed in Europe, USA, Canada, Australia, Japan

Cover: Foto ©Raphael Reischuk / pixelio.de

More available books at **www.hansebooks.com**

A MEMORIAL SKETCH

OF

LIEUT. EDGAR M. NEWCOMB,

OF THE

NINETEENTH MASS. VOLS.

———

EDITED BY DR. A. B. WEYMOUTH.

———

Printed for Private Distribution.

————⊷•⊷ - - -

MALDEN:

ALVIN G. BROWN, STEAM BOOK AND JOB PRINTER.

1883.

INTRODUCTORY REMARKS.

"They arose, all the valiant men."—I Chron. x, 12.

More than twenty years have passed away since the heroic dead of Fredericksburg entered into rest. Why record the story of their sufferings? Or, if the "oft-repeated tale" must be again recited, why distinguish between the loyal men who fell at Fredericksburg, and equally-devoted patriots who met the last enemy on other fields? To these questions the only possible answer is that this biographical record was undertaken as a labor of love, in tribute to the memory of an intimate friend. The long-deferred personal sketch in the following pages is not intended for the perusal of the public, and need not occupy the attention of readers who have no interest in the scenes narrated. The sad story of Fredericksburg is, in many respects, peculiar, and perhaps no other conflict during the rebellion rests under the shadow of so dark a cloud. Its silver lining is so narrow as to be almost imperceptible to finite vision.

The world has never seen better soldiers than those composing the Army of the Potomac. Brilliant genius, metal culture, sublime patriotism, dauntless courage, and inflexible purpose were in many instances conspicuous in the ranks, as well as among the commissioned officers. The best young men of the nation were found in the ranks of blue. The character of our noble defenders will be more correctly appreciated after a study of individual reminiscences. Very imperfectly and briefly, the life-work of a gallant young soldier will be narrated. Scattered memorial gems have been collected from various sources, with the hope that their intrinsic beauty may secure their preservation. No effort has been made to increase their natural lustre. Rhetorical ornament has been intentionally avoided. Indispensable assistance has been rendered by relatives of our hero, and also by several of his companions-in-arms. Special acknowledgement of favors received is due to Colonel John C. Chadwick, Major H. G. O. Weymouth, Captain Stephen I. Newman, Captain William A. Hill, Captain J. G. B. Adams, John L. Robinson, formerly clerk at head-quarters, 19th Regiment, George H. Patch, Past Commander Mass. Dept., G. A. R., and Charles A. Newhall, secretary of the 19th Regiment Association. Indulgence is craved for all defects and errors.

CHILDHOOD AND SCHOOL DAYS.

" With us his name shall live,
 Through long succeeding years,
 Embalmed, with all our hearts can give—
 Our praises and our tears."

A MEMORIAL SKETCH

OF

LIEUT. EDGAR M. NEWCOMB,

OF THE NINETEENTH MASS. VOLS.

EDGAR MARSHALL NEWCOMB, eldest son of John Jay and Mary Starbuck (Marshall) Newcomb, was born in the city of Troy, N. Y., on October 2, 1840. From the excellent geneology published by the Hon. John B. Newcomb, of Elgin, Ill., it appears that the family was in possession of ancestral seats at Saltfleetby, Lincolnshire, Eng., 700 years ago. Latin records in the parish church commence in 1558. Captain Andrew Newcomb emigrated from the west of England to this country with some of the early colonists. He was in Boston in 1663, and three years later imported horses and other animals. In 1679 he was "master of ye sloope Edmund & Martha," at the port of New York, bound for Boston. He probably sailed from Virginia, as a portion of his cargo was tobacco. His house was in Boston, near the "mill bridge." On January 31, 1682, he executed a will, making his grandchild, Newcomb Blake, executor. Until the grandchild should become of age, Samuel Marshall of Boston was appointed executor in trust. For his services in taking care of the estate, Mr. Marshall received a small legacy. Thus we notice friendly relations existing between the Newcomb and Marshall families more than two hundred years ago.

Lieut. Andrew Newcomb, son of the Captain, was at the Isles of Shoals in 1666. He removed to Martha's Vineyard in 1675, and became one of the proprietors of Edgartown. He held the office of constable and other positions of trust; was commissioned Lieutenant on April 13, 1691, and in the same year became commander of the fortification which defended the harbor. The name given to the settlement, and the rank of the highest military officer, remind us of his descendant, whose history is recorded in the following pages.

Simon Newcomb, a son of the Lieutenant, removed to Edgartown with his father, and subsequently to Lebanon, Conn., where he died in January, 1744. He was an excellent man and owned considerable property. Thomas Newcomb, son of Simon, was born at Edgartown in 1691, and carried on an extensive mercantile business at Salisbury, Conn. He was a member of the church at Lebanon, and afterwards at Salisbury. His death occurred in 1761. Zaccheus Newcomb, son of Thomas, was born at Lebanon in 1724. After attaining his majority he removed to Pleasant Valley, Duchess Co., N. Y. He served in the Revolutionary War, and while he was in the army his wife built a fine brick house, which remains to this day. It is said that she presented General Washington and the British Commander with cheeses from her own dairy.

John Newcomb, son of the Revolutionary patriot, was born at Pleasant Valley, N. Y., on March 1, 1770. In 1791 he married Ruth, daughter of Judge Isaac Bloom. He inherited 300 acres of land in Albany County. One of his sons, Isaac B. Newcomb, married Julia Marshall and removed to Annandale, Fairfax County, Va. When the Rebellion broke out, he was arrested on account of his well-known Union sentiments, and died a prisoner of war at Libby prison, in November, 1861. Another son of John Newcomb, is Mr. John Jay Newcomb, of Boston. His native place was Pleasant Valley, N. Y. While residing at Troy, N. Y., in October, 1837, Mr. J. J. Newcomb married Mary Starbuck, daughter of Benjamin S. and Maria (Starbuck) Marshall. During the war of 1812 Mrs. Newcomb's father was captured at sea, and was one of the Dartmoor prisoners. One of her ancestors was a distinguished officer of high rank in the navy. For a short time Mr. and Mrs. Newcomb resided at Toledo, O., where their first child, Leila Antoinette, was born. This darling daughter died when 3 years of age. The birth of Edgar, the oldest son, is recorded above. When he was about six months old, Mr. and Mrs. Newcomb removed to Boston, Mass., where they still reside. A daughter (Leila Frances) and three sons (Charles Benjamin, John Jay and James Gifford) were born in Boston.

Edgar was a healthy child, although his constitution was rather delicate. He was tenderly nurtured, and received his primary education at home. In childhood and youth he was in great measure shielded from external influences which usually tend to develope the rudeness of boyish nature. He was a bright and clever lad, with handsome features of almost feminine delicacy, refined in his disposition and deportment, studious and in all respects exemplary. He instinctively discerned the poetic and beautiful in nature and art. The child of Christian parents he was fond of meditating upon the high themes of destiny, and at the early age of eleven years consecrated himself to a religious life; ever seeking to perform duty—the noble idea which in after years inspired his soldierly career.

Soon after this important and pivotal point in his history, it was deemed advisable to place him under public instruction, and accordingly he entered the Adams Grammar School, on Mason street, Boston, and remained a pupil of this school for six months. In September, 1852, Edgar was admitted a member of the fourth class in the Public Latin School, on Bedford street. The Rev. Henry F. Jenks, in his history of the school, declared it to be "the oldest educational institution in the country. Its first masters might have seen Shakespeare act in his own plays. * * A preparatory school should naturally be established before a college: So it is not strange that this school antedates Harvard College by two or three years, justifying the remark of a distinguished graduate of both, that 'the Latin School dandled Harvard College on her knees'. The establishment of this school is largely due to John Cotton, who brought to this country a knowledge of the High School which was founded by Philip and Mary in 1554, in Boston, in Lincolnshire, England, in which Latin and Greek were taught. Cotton came to this country in 1633, and was one of the ministers of the First Church. Two years later, the Free School was established." The school-house on Bedford street was the fourth building erected for the time-honored school, and this substantial edifice has recently ceased to exist, the school removing to a structure of almost palatial elegance on Warren avenue.

Francis Gardner, for a long period a faithful instructor in the school, had been appointed principal shortly before young Newcomb became a pupil. The regular course of study at this period occupied six years; but Master Gardner quickly discerning Edgar's superior talents, encouraged him to make extra exertions and complete the prescribed studies in four years. This advice was cheerfully accepted, and our diligent friend, with commendable ambition, toiled early and late at his daily task. Such unwearied application to study was not without gratifying results, for his carefully-prepared lessons were uniformly recited with credit.

Near the close of his course at the Latin School, several members of the class requested permission to visit the Charlestown Navy Yard on the day appointed for the launching of the Merrimac, the famous vessel which was afterwards transformed into a Confederate iron-clad ram, at Norfolk, Va. Edgar was as interested in the event as any of his classmates, but preferred to remain at school, regarding study as a duty not to be neglected. One of his letters, printed on a subsequent page, records his impressions on board an army transport, near the scene of the desperate naval engagement between the Merrimac and the Monitor—the first terrific encounter between ironclad vessels in the history of the world.

Newcomb's kindness and inclination to serve others will appear from the following incidents. Once a year, during vacation, Master Gardner was accustomed to examine and re-arrange the books and engravings in the library of the Latin School Association. On these occasions he was aided by a few of his pupils who volunteered their services; Edgar was more than once among the number, considering it no hardship to work all day, while his schoolmates were spending their time in idleness or recreation.

The sessions of the school were five hours in length, from 9 A. M. to 2 P. M., and during recess in summer the boys sometimes desired a cooling beverage. In order to supply the wants of his intimate friends, Newcomb obtained permission to visit his home

—at that time on Essex street, not far from the schoolhouse—for the purpose of preparing lemonade and other palatable refreshments. For these services he at first declined to receive any remuneration, and never would take more than the actual cost.

Acting according to the promptings of a laudable ambition, Newcomb once or twice engaged in the competition for the Lawrence prizes, and his efforts bore fruitage in honorable rewards. On May 26, 1855, he received a prize "for a poetical translation from Virgil." Some amusement was caused by the occurrence of a misprint in the catalogue, stating that the prize was for a "practical translation from Virgil." The Rev. Will C. Wood of Scituate, Mass., a class-mate whose memory is rarely at fault, writes as follows: "I am quite confident he also had a prize for good conduct or scholarship."

About this period Edgar made a public declaration of his Christian faith by becoming a member of Park Street church. A portion of the records of this church were destroyed in the great Boston fire in 1872, and consequently the exact date cannot be given. Several friends made profession of religion at the same time, and the occasion was a joyful one in the highest sense.

In the course of his last term at the Latin School Newcomb made a spirited translation of a passage from a Greek funeral oration, in memory of soldiers who died for their country. The good seed of patriotism fell into good ground, and afterwards yielded abundant increase.

Exercises in elocution very properly held a prominent place in the studies of the school. On a well-remembered "Public Saturday," in the presence of a large audience, Edgar's declamation was particularly impressive and thrilling. His selection on that day was "The Soldier from Bingen," and his interpretation of the plaintive utterances of the dying soldier-lad was extremely touching. Was it prophetic of his own glorious destiny?

[When he was only seven years old another remarkable incident occurred, apparently fore-ordained with relation to coming events. In company with his parents he visited Fairfax, Va., and gazed upon the Court House which he was afterwards called upon to defend amid the vicissitudes of fratricidal war. Reflections upon this occasion will be found in one of his letters on a subsequent page.]

On July 12, 1856, the graduating exercises of Newcomb's class were held in the exhibition hall of the Latin School. The following account is taken from the *Boston Journal:* " As the oldest classical institution in the country, and the crowning glory of the public schools of this city, all its public days are deserving of attention. On this occasion the attendance was large, and the audience appeared to be highly gratified. The exercises commenced with an examination of the several classes in the studies of the past year. In these the young gentlemen showed evidence of careful study and training, and a degree of proficiency worthy the high reputation of the school. Next in order the members of the graduating class delivered their 'parts' in a satisfactory manner. The speaking in most cases was of a high order, especially that of the prize boys." Edgar's part was an excellent "Poetical Translation from Ovid." His natural gifts as a poet were manifested in a degree which was quite remarkable for one of his years.

COLLEGE LIFE AND EUROPEAN TOUR.

"Much study is a weariness of the flesh,"—ECCLESIASTES XII, 12.

A few days after graduating from the Latin School, New-comb was admitted a member of the freshman class of Harvard College, passing the examinations with brilliant success. In company with one of his classmates at the Latin School, (Frederic William Batchelder), he engaged rooms at the residence of Mr. J. S. Bates, No 15 Hilliard street, (a few minutes' walk from the college grounds in Old Cambridge) where he remained two years. The Holmes school-house was erected on the lot directly opposite, a few years ago. From Hilliard street it is nearly a straight line, through Appian way, to the soldiers' monument on Cambridge common. Throughout the college course Edgar boarded with his parents at No. 56 Worcester street, Boston, where the family still resides. When the weather was pleasant he often walked from Cambridge to Boston in the evening, softly singing, "I'm a Pilgrim," "Homeward Bound," and other sacred melodies. "For he looked for a city which hath foundations, whose builder and maker is God."

One or two summer vacations were spent at Watertown, Mass., and our young friend experienced great pleasure in visiting the United States arsenal on the banks of the Charles. Here again we notice an apparent foreshadowing of his military career. Although his intrepid nature and innate heroism were usually concealed beneath a quiet exterior, intimate friends now and then caught glimpses of these martial qualities in his juvenile sports. In a few instances Newcomb surprised some of his classmates by exhibiting boldness in forming his plans, and steadiness in carrying them into execution. His associates had never dreamed that daring qualities were inherent in his mental constitution, and regard for their own safety prevented any attempt at imitation. In after years, as the reader will discover, this rare trait of true courage was manifested amid scenes of carnage which appalled even veteran troops; and Newcomb was often found at the front when the shafts of death were falling fast on every side.

Our friend was zealous in the performance of religious duty, but his piety was never of a gloomy and repellent character. No young man more heartily enjoyed the lawful and innocent pleasures of earth. Edgar possessed the happy faculty of blending Christianity with the common affairs of life, and even with his recreations. His good-natured pleasantry was noticeable on all proper occasions, and his merry laugh will not soon be forgotten. In social circles his ready wit and genial smile made him the centre of attraction. He was particularly skilled in the game of chess, and saw no impropriety in mingling observations upon the highest themes with the manœuvring of pieces upon the board. While vanquishing an opponent in this intricate pastime he occasionally secured a double victory by pressing theological conclusions with irresistible logic.

During the second half of the college course our diligent student occupied room No. 20 in Graduates' Hall. This building was afterwards enlarged as the necessities of the University required, and is now known as College House. F. W. Batchelder and C. A. Nelson were Newcomb's "chums" during the junior year, and D. T. S. Leland was his room-mate during the senior year. Other friends were frequently entertained at "G. 20," and the remembrance of those days is exceedingly pleasant.

Newcomb was an active member of the "Ydell Cruth," one of the societies which was "organized by and passed out of existence with the class" of 1860. In July, 1859, he delivered before the society a beautiful poem, which is given below.

ZOROASTER'S VISION.

Ages before the morning stars had sung,
Or angel's praise through heaven's high arches rung,
Awful the stillness when through space alone,
Wrapt in eternal light, shone Allah's throne.
But grander yet the moment when before
That mighty throne stood two, whose image bore

The impress of their God, whose adverse sway
Must ever part the universe to be.
One, radiant with the light which ever streamed
From Allah's self, the soul of goodness seemed.
Worthy the source divine from which he sprung,
Worthy the anthems of immortal song.
His brother, frowning as the black of night,
Shrouded in stormy clouds his equal might,
And, flashing hate from out the deepening gloom,
Bespoke a demon's rage, a demon's home.

Ages rolled on ; and angel choirs had sung
The latest blessing Ormusd's hand had given,—
A new-born world which round his footstool swung,
Suspended by a silver cord from heaven.
The dust that lay on the celestial floor
Lighted and cheered its seraph messengers,
And sweetly broke on its eternal shore
The faint exquisite music of the spheres.
But brighter shines that new-created star,
Illumining the dusky realms of space,
And sweeter than the notes of angels are,
Rises the incense of her morning praise.
Silent and swift, the chariot of the sun
Circles the planet on its shining way,
And night, in trailing garments, follows on,
Fringing her skirts with his declining ray.
The rain-drop falls upon her fertiled breast,
And springs again in beauteous drapery,—
The purpling cluster, or the golden crest
Of harvest plenty, or the olive tree.
The woodland kings, lifting their arms on high,
Applaud with myriad bands the rosy morn :
And Flora's realms, in blushing ecstasy,
The fragrant kisses of the breeze return ;
While animate creation lends the voice
Of its dumb eloquence to swell the song,
The gushing tribute of ten thousand joys
Whose grateful utterance makes those joys more strong.
But, last and best of all earth's creatures, man,
Immortal image of the Eternal One ;
And woman's love that broke and joined again
The link that bound her home to Ormusd's throne.

Ye seraphs, adore him who swings in the skies
The censer whose perfumes so sweetly arise.
O children of earth, in the joy of your morning,
Resound ye the praise of the infinite Lord,
Who has set in the realms of heaven's adorning
This emerald gem by the might of his word.

Rejoice, for the choirs of heaven descending
Illumine the earth and the dwellings of men;
And angels, with mortals in harmony blending.
Waft upward the notes of their chanting again.
Jehovah comes down from the throne of his glory
To talk with his creatures and order their song ;
Oh, ages, repeat the delectable story ;
And. heaven, the tale of its mercy prolong.
Ye seraphs, adore him who swings in the skies
The censer whose perfumes so sweetly arise.

Then Ahriman arrays his evil band :
Unseen and silently their footsteps fall.
Till on the utmost bound of earth they stand
And eager plot their hellish carnival,
The sun shone brightly on the fields of earth,
The songs of joy still rolled along her vales,
And nature knew not of the evil birth
Which time, alas! too fearfully reveals.
A demon breathes upon the harvest grain,
And blighting mildew rots its golden fruit,
And quickly follow in their hateful train,
To feast upon its wealth with fierce dispute,
The noisy insect and the loathsome worm.
He treads the earth, and from his footsteps spring
The nettle's thorny spike, and every form
That demon skill could work of bane or sting :
The yew and cypress hang their mournful heads,
The Upas-tree distils its deadly ooze,
And even now, as fall the evening shades,
Earth tells her sorrows in the falling dews.
A demon points the serpent's fatal fang,
And bids him hiss along his slimy way ;
A demon teaches well the lions tongue
To drink the life-blood of a human prey.
The Sun draws near in his meridian blaze
To scorch earth's bosom with his summer heat ;
Then leaves her to deplore his distant rays.
Wrapt in the chill of winter's winding sheet ;
And nature's self, trembling in helpless pride.
And deeply moaning in her agony,
Pours her wild grief adown the mountain-side,
Till its hot streams are stifled in the sea.
But, last and greatest of her myriad woes—
The cherished work of the Arch Fiend alone—
Man, sinning, falls, and woman only knows
To yield her love and blindly follow on.

Let the seraphim cease in this sounding of praise,
For the wailings of sorrow have reached to the skies.

Sweet was the brightness of earth's sunny morning
E'er the tempter had clouded the sky of her joy,
And dark is the night that now utters its warning,
When their mission is ended who came to destroy.
Ye children of men, let the light of your dwelling
Be darkened, and hushed be the voice of your song;
For the wrath that has followed your faithless rebelling
Shall deepen its course as it hurries along.
Bewail, for the choirs of heaven ascending,
In sorrow, have fled the pollution of men;
And over the heavenly battlements bending,
In sorrow look back on earth's beauty again.
Jehovah no more from the throne of his glory
Descends to the homes of his children below;
No more will their voices repeat the glad story,
And the choirs of heaven its harmony know.
Let the Seraphim cease in their chanting of praise,
For the wailings of sorrow have reached to the skies.

Thus ends Part I. of this poem, which speaks for itself and requires no praise. It bears silent testimony to the remarkable gifts of the composer. Illness prevented the completion of Part II. In his last year at Cambridge our poet became a member of another College society—the Christian Brethren—which is still in a flourishing condition. When circumstances would permit, he attended its meetings and other religious gatherings.

Early in the senior year Newcomb developed a taste which at first surprised his friends. As far as is known he never expressed an intention of entering the medical profession. Yet he accepted with evident satisfaction an invitation to visit the Massachusetts General Hospital. For a number of weeks in succession he visited the institution, and witnessed the surgical operations with attention and interest, subsequently describing the treatment with remarkable accuracy. Beneath that venerable dome, in the operating room where ether was first administered in capital operations, Newcomb renewed his acquaintance with Josiah N. Willard who had nearly finished his medical studies. Seven years previous to this date they studied the classics in Master Gardner's room at the Latin School, Willard's class being three years in advance. At Cambridge, they occasionally exchanged greetings during Willard's senior year. In the operating theatre Willard was happy to explain the points most attractive to a tyro in medical science. Less than two years after the hospital interviews their paths again converged, and they met upon the tented field as members of the same regiment. When the Nineteenth Regiment, Mass. Vols., was organized, Dr. Willard was commissioned Assistant Surgeon. During active service, Newcomb frequently devoted his spare moments to the relief of the sick and wounded. The under-graduate's strange predilection for hospital scenes was Providentially intended as a preparation for usefulness amid the horrors of war. If we are surrounded with mystery and uncertainty, let us confidently hope for a satisfactory explanation—here or hereafter.

The words of the wise ruler, quoted at the commencement of this chapter, proved true in the case of our friend before the college curriculum came to a close. Much study induced physical weakness and nervous prostration. Long continued mental application became impossible, and efforts to secure university honors were discontinued. Still the ambitious student performed more work than was advisable under the circumstances, a change of scene became an imperative duty, and a voyage to Europe was recommended by the family physician.

Before bidding adieu to the university, perhaps it may not seem out of place to present the reflections and observations of some surviving members of Newcomb's class, written years after his decease. The Rev. James C. Fernald, in the "Harvard Memorial Biographies," writes as follows: "In person Lieut. Newcomb was above the medium height, with well-proportioned figure, pleasing features and a complexion of feminine fairness. * * His college course was more prominently marked by the unusual rectitude and purity of his life—and by a religious activity, earnest without ostensiveness or arrogance—than by high intellectual triumphs. These were, indeed, precluded by the state of his health. * * His military career was of a peculiar type. There were elements latent in his character which needed only the touch of duty and danger to make him conspicuous among the brave. * * The enthusiastic valor he displayed was a surprise to many." Other classmates express their appreciation of his character in similar terms.

The following passage occurs in a letter written by Dr.

Franklin Nickerson, of Lowell: "I feel sure that I should simply be bearing testimony to what you perhaps know more fully, in any attempt that I should make to describe our hero, for true hero he was as I believe, throughout life. The Procrustean recitation room did not give him scope for that display of the higher qualities of his nature which the broader field of life afforded. We little thought that Shaw and Newcomb, both alike quiet and unobtrusive as they were in their boyhood, would turn out to be such men of action and leave behind them an immortal record. I think Newcomb's life was of the highest type. One trait of his character shone forth with great strength through his modest retirement of manner, and that was moral courage. He was head and shoulders above most of his fellows in this respect. He was one of the few of our number who could rise superior to the temptations of student life."

The Rev. Will C. Wood, of Scituate, Mass., gives the following testimony: "Newcomb I remember as a hearty, cheerful, noble fellow. Strangely I think of him more than in any other locality in Mount Auburn. One of the walks and times there you will recollect." Dr. Francis M. Weld, of New York city, secretary of the class of 1860, also refers to Mount Auburn "in whose sacred precincts Newcomb delighted, when at Cambridge, to seclude himself for study and meditation."

Limited space requires that college reminiscences should be brought to a close. Contemplating a prolonged sojourn across the sea, Edgar wrote to a relative as follows: "I shall often think of you in my absence, and always as of one growing in grace, and learning daily that the Christian life-work is to supply defects and correct the perverted working of our own faculties, rather than watch the development of graces already in existence."

Shortly before commencement in 1860, Newcomb engaged passage for Europe in the bark "Lawrence," sailing from St. John, N. B. The captain's wife was also a passenger. After a pleasant voyage Edgar landed in England, but soon had the misfortune to lose his baggage, letters of introduction and most of his money. Determined to continue his journey as long as possible, the undaunted and persevering traveller reduced his expenses by a pedestrian excursion through a portion of England and France.

On arriving at Paris he had only sixty cents left, and wisely sought the advice of the American Consul. In this time of need he was thankful to meet Mr. Clark, a valued friend whom he afterwards met in the army, and an acquaintance who was formerly a member of the Harvard Law School. Newcomb's knowledge of French was found very useful in Paris. A thorough drill in this language at the Latin School in Boston imparted much more than the smattering of the Gallic tongue commonly at the command of our countrymen in France. While walking the streets of Paris, our friend became the guide of two English gentlemen who were unable to speak a word of French. They recognized not only his usefulness in this capacity, but his agreeable manners, superior intelligence and excellent education. They requested his company on a trip to Versailles, but the invitation was courteously declined. The gentlemen insisted upon knowing some good reason for the refusal, and Edgar frankly admitted that he could not afford the expense. The generous Englishmen offered ten pounds sterling, and secured his valuable services as interpreter and companion. In the midst of his pecuniary misfortunes Newcomb wrote to a Mr. Walton at whose house he had stopped while in London. Mr. Walton, knowing instinctively that the young American was perfectly trustworthy, promptly sent a small remittance. Thinking it was imprudent to proceed further with such slender resources, Edgar returned to England and engaged passage in a sailing vessel bound for New York.

Arriving home late in the autumn, the health of our traveller was considerably improved, but still he was not sufficiently vigorous for a regular course of professional training, and his cherished expectation of commencing theological studies was indefinitely postponed. To one possessing his active temperament idleness would be an impossibility, and he gladly accepted a position as clerk in his father's counting room on Commerce street, Boston. Mr. John J. Newcomb carried on an extensive business as commission merchant, dealing largely in flour, pork and other staple commodities. Edgar soon became familiar with the routine of business at the store, collected bills, attended to financial transactions at the banks, and superintended the shipment of merchandise. On Sundays and Friday evenings he was never absent from church. As an avocation he frequently engaged in theological, literary and political discussions with intimate acquaintances. Soon after the triumph of the Republican party, resulting in the election of Abraham Lincoln to the presidency, Edgar recognized the fact that war was inevitable.

MARTIAL ECHOES.

"Thou therefore endure hardness, as a good soldier of Jesus Christ."—2 TIM. II, 3.

> " Our native land to thee,
> In one united vow,
> To keep thee strong and free
> And glorious as now—
> We pledge each heart and hand.
> By the blood our fathers shed,
> By the ashes of our dead,
> By the sacred soil we tread,
> God for our native land."
> GEORGE W. BETHUNE.

Early in May, 1861, as an obedient son of a New England home, Edgar asked his mother this important question: "Mother, would you be willing to let me go to the war?" The loyal lady replied, " Yes; and I would go myself, if I could." No serious obstacle being in the way, our patriotic young citizen during leisure hours prepared himself daily for his country's service by private military drill, becoming quite proficient in the manual of arms. After the first disaster to the national cause at Bull Run, he made this remark to a classmate: "I felt so ashamed at the result that I could not look any one in the face." More than once Edgar visited camps of instruction at Lynnfield, Readville and elsewhere. After an interview with a student friend who had already enlisted at great personal sacrifice, Newcomb determined to do likewise at the first favorable opportunity. His decision was almost inevitable under the circumstances. Sentiments of patriotism and loyalty were powerfully stimulated. Military enthusiasm had heretofore been a slumbering element in Edgar's nature, and it was fully aroused by the national call to arms. We have seen that one of his ancestors was a Lieutenant in 1691. Another direct ancestor was a Revolutionary soldier. His Grandfather, (on his mother's side,) had suffered in the war of 1812. The Newcombs in America may justly claim to be a martial family; 21 members of the family served in wars before the Revolution; 71 in the Revolutionary war; 71 in the war of 1812: 7 in the Mexican war; 225 on the Union side in the war of the Rebellion. Several of these patriots attained high rank, and all of them were faithful soldiers. "Prowess eminent," like other mental characteristics, may be inherited in some degree.

CAMP AT LYNNFIELD.

At this time Newcomb was boarding with his relatives at a stately mansion overlooking Barrett's pond, in Malden, Mass. One of his visits to Camp Schouler, at Lynnfield, during the second or third week of August, 1861, was unusually prolonged, leading his parents to suspect that their son could no longer refrain from carrying his noble purpose into execution. Returning, the next day, Edgar requested a confidential interview with Mrs. Newcomb and said: "Mother I am going away tomorrow," and his mother's consent given in May was not retracted. Accordingly, on the following morning he left for Lynnfield, entered the camp of the Nineteenth Mass. Vols., and offered his services to Captain Edmund Rice (a gentleman with whom he was somewhat acquainted), then in command of company F. This excellent officer advised his recruit not to be mustered into the United States' service until the regiment was about to leave for the front. Captain Rice kindly introduced Newcomb to a congenial comrade of refined and gentlemanly tastes, E. G. Manning, of North Andover. This exemplary young man rose from the ranks, and eventually attained the rank of Captain in another regiment. Newcomb's relatives visited the camp, and he was allowed to spend the following Sabbath at home.

A large number of Essex County men enlisted in the Nineteenth regiment. During the three months' service at the commencement of the war, the Eighth regiment was commanded by Colonel Edward W. Hinks, of Lynn, who has the reputation of being the first man who offered his services for the war. On his return to Massachusetts the gallant Colonel was instructed to assume command of the Nineteenth Mass. Vols., enlisted for three years. The regiment was ordered to leave the State on Wednes day, August 28. The Daily Evening *Transcript* of that date contains the following: "The Nineteenth regiment, Col. Hinks, which has been in camp at Lynnfield for several weeks, will leave for the seat of war this afternoon. The camp will be broken up and the tents struck at three o'clock, and the troops come to Boston by the way of Salem, over the Eastern Railroad, reaching the city about five. They go to New York by the Fall River route, and will leave the depot of the Old Colony Railroad at seven o'clock. The following is the roster of the regiment:

Colonel—Edward W. Hinks, Lynn.
Lieutenant Colonel—Arthur F. Devereau, Salem.
Major—Henry J. How, Haverhill.
Surgeon—J. Franklin Dyer, Rockport.
Assistant Surgeon—Josiah N. Willard, Boston.
Adjutant—John C. Chadwick, Salem.
Quartermaster—Levi Shaw, Rockport.

Co. A, Captain, Moses P. Stanwood, West Newbury; 1st Lieut., Charles M. Merritt, Lynn; 2nd Lieut., Isaac H. Boyd, West Newbury.

Co. B, Captain, Elijah P. Rogers, West Newbury; 1st Lieut., John Hodges, Jr., Salem; 2d Lieut., James T. Lurvey, Lowell.

Co. C, Captain, J. Scott Todd, Rowley; 1st Lieut., George W. Batchelder, Salem; 2d Lieut., Samuel S. Prime, Rowley.

Co. D, Captain, James D. Russell, Boston; 1st Lieut., Moneena Dunn, Boston; 2d Lieut., John P. Reynolds, Jr., Salem.

Co. E, Captain, Andrew Mahoney, Boston; 1st Lieut., David Lee, Boston; 2d Lieut., George M. Barry, Boston.

Co. F, Captain, Edmund Rice, Cambridge; 1st Lieut., James H. Rice, Brighton; 2d Lieut., James G. C. Dodge, Boston.

Co. G, Captain, Harrison G. O. Weymouth, Lowell; 1st Lieut., Samuel D. Hovey, Lowell; 2d Lieut., Dudley C. Mumford, Lowell.

Co. H, Captain, William H. Wilson, Roxbury; 1st Lieut., Henry A. Hale, Salem; 2d Lieut., Wm. H. Lecain, Boston.

Co. I, Captain, Jonathan F. Plympton, Boston; 1st Lieut., Christopher C. Sampson, Boston; 2d Lieut., Wm. L. Palmer, Salem.

Co. K, Captain, Ansel D. Wass, Boston; 1st Lieut., Eugene Kelty, Boston; 2d Lieut., Edward P. Bishop, Boston."

DEPARTURE OF THE 19th REGIMENT.

On Wednesday, Aug. 28, 1861, promptly at the hour appointed, the regiment was ready to leave for the front. Full particulars will be found in Newcomb's letter dated Sept. 1, 1861. The Nineteenth came to Boston by way of Salem, as stated in the newspaper paragraph. According to a previous arrangement, when the regiment marched up State street, Boston, Newcomb's friends were at a prominent corner, and his mother gave this parting admonition : "Edgar, be a good boy." On marching through the city, the weight of equipments which each soldier was obliged to carry was no small burden to the strongest, and our friend's physical strength was hardly equal to the task. When the regiment arrived at the parade ground on Boston Common a halt was ordered, and the men were allowed to rest for about two hours and a half. Mr. and Mrs. Newcomb were unaware of this circumstance, and consequently lost an opportunity for further conversation with their son. Lieutenant (afterward Captain) James H. Rice, comments as follows: "It was a very trying experience for us all, the command being in heavy marching order, and the day being very warm. Newcomb was of slight physique, and I have no doubt he was much exhausted, as were many others, by the march and heat."

On the following day, the regiment arrived in New York city. A telegraphic despatch, given below, was published in the Boston *Journal:* "New York, Thursday, Aug. 29. The Massachusetts 19th regiment arrived via Fall River boat, at 2 o'clock this afternoon, and proceeded to Park barracks, where dinner was provided by Assistant Quarter-master Frank E. Howe." Charles B. Newcomb, a young brother, was at this time in New York city on business, and the joyful meeting of Charles and Edgar can well be imagined. Early on Friday morning, Aug. 30, the regiment reached Philadelphia. After a short rest the journey was resumed, no serious difficulty occured during the march through Baltimore, and the 19th arrived at Washington after midnight.

CAMP AT MERIDIAN HILL, NEAR WASHINGTON.

On Saturday afternoon Colonel Hinks received orders to march to Meridian hill, near the city. Here the regiment was allowed to encamp and rest for a week or two. The following letter from Newcomb gives interesting details.

WASHINGTON, 1ST SEPT., 1861.

DEAREST SISTER:

Here I am at last, within ten miles or less of the enemy's pickets. We struck tents Tuesday last at Lynnfield, passing the night in the open air. Privates slept on the ground; I, being Corporal, slep. on a board. Wednesday morning we received two days' rations, i. e., four sandwiches or eight crackers, and four pieces of ham. Expecting to go at 3 p. m., we were ordered to "harness up" about 2, but as we did not take the train till 4½, our knapsacks &c., became very heavy long before that. At last, after much marching and standing in the hot sun, we went aboard the cars. As we started, every man shouted and almost screamed for joy, and continued it till we reached Boston. They cheered for the Captain and Lieutenants, for the girls that sal. uted them as they passed, for the gun that boomed out as we reached and left Salem, and last for a potato-digger who stared at us as we passed. At 5 we reached Boston and marched to the Common. Having seen you in State street, I did not expect to do so on the Common, but I met some dozen friends. We remained on the Common, all harnessed and waiting for orders, till 8¼ p. m.; when our officers having returned from supper, we marched to the Old Colony Railroad. At 2, Thursday a. m., we left Fall River; and here the privations of the Regiment generally, and of Co. F especially, began. Being the flank company, we came last aboard and were stowed in the steerage. The company before us had taken the berths even of this, and we slept on the floor. Fatigue overcame noise, and amid the talking and tramping around and above me, I slept almost without interruption until 8 the next morning. I woke up stiff and cold, and having no taste for hard bread, tried to buy of the cooks or darkies, but only the officers could be supplied, and I must go hungry. I found a man who sold mince pies and various drinks, and, not daring to try the former, I bought a glass of mineral water, but going a short time after into the steerage, it with the foul air and an empty stomach made me so sick that I was permitted to put my baggage in the wagon, and since then I have travelled quite easily. Thursday noon we reached New York, and Co. F must stand guard. I thought it would be easier than marching and offered myself, but was refused because I was sick.

Again I offered, as I hoped to see Charlie, and another officer received me. As the guard filed out from the steamboat, Charlie saw and met me, and all day long we were alone together on a transport, while the rest of our company stood guard and sweated under their knapsacks, when the regiment halted on its hot and weary march through enthusiastic and hospitable New York. In the evening the transport went to Amboy where I slept on the deck till the regiment arrived, and here I bade Charlie good-bye. His generosity and love had fed me in the morning with bread, tea and peaches, and filled my haversack at night with bread and beef steak. I felt far better because I had enjoyed his society for the day. We reached Philadelphia about 3½ Friday morning, and marched to the barracks established for the refreshment of soldiers; enjoyed an early breakfast and excellent. Thus far Boston alone had given her own children nothing to eat, and her farewell was least hearty and touching. As we left Philadelphia at 5, few men were awake, but from here to Ferryville we were everywhere met with the most enthusiastic welcome. And touching it was, that our cause was so dear and sacred to the hearts of the multitude, that its defenders whom they had never seen before were treated so tenderly and generously. We marched through Baltimore 1½ miles, and were cheered twice only; once by three persons led by a U. S. soldier. From Baltimore to Washington we rode in cattle-cars, and arrived at the latter place about 12½ p. m. We stood under arms in the dark till 2 Saturday a. m., when we were marched in to a collation of fat and stinking bacon, sour bread and pea coffee. I drank a few swallows of coffee, and returned to find that our company and one other were to sleep on a platform outside the building where the rest of the regiment slept under cover. Fearing something of the sort, I had obtained from a fellow soldier the promise of his woollen blanket (my own was in the baggage waggon,) and having procured it I lay down on the rough planks and slept till late in the morning. We were marched in to breakfast on the same fare as the night before, but the soldiers (impatient at having gone for 60 hours with but two fair meals when Uncle Sam provided for us so bountifully, and then insulted by such rations) threw them at one another and at the waiters. Next day the Colonel came to examine the bacon, and threw it across the room. When dinner came we fared better than before, but a second visit convinced us of his desire to do us justice, and the caterers of his disgust and indignation at our treatment. In the afternoon we marched three miles to our encampment on a hill well-wooded, from which we can see the country for miles around. The Potomac is 1½ miles distant, and the whole country most delightful. We have now fair rations, and sleep in tents; but there have been no services to-day, and as I heard the church-bells of Washington ringing, and thought that it was communion Sabbath at home, I felt most deeply the deprivations of these blessings. Since last Monday I have neither changed my clothes nor read my Bible till to-day. I greatly enjoy myself nevertheless, and, but for a bad cold, am far better than usual. I havn't suffered from hunger since I arrived at New York, for there are very few places where that which answereth all things is of no avail. I have become acquainted with Lewis who is Adjutant's clerk. He has interested himself in me, but whether his friendship will amount to anything I do not know. All the company officers and many of the men seem especially kind to me, but if I thought my position other than temporary, I could not enjoy myself. In your answer to this letter tell me all about Ed. Hall's enlisting and how he procured his commission; where he is, and how he feels. There is nothing more of interest, and hereafter there will not be usually so much as this letter contains—camp life is so monotonous and devoid of "spice." Give my love to everybody. Tell everybody to write me, as, whenever I have time, all letters shall be readily answered. Direct in care Capt. Rice, Co. F, 19th Reg., Washington.

EDGAR.

The extract given below is taken from a letter written on the same day by Knights, a member of the regiment who occasionally acted as war correspondent of the Gloucester (Mass.) Telegraph : "The difference between our muster and rendezvous camps at home and an encampment of troops on service, never seemed to me so distinctly marked as it appears today ; and we are comparatively distant from the enemy. The hurrying to and fro of officers and squads of men,—the ringing of axes, lumbering of wagons, and the shouts of the wagoners,— the smoke of camp-fires, the frequent drum-beat and bugle-call,— all these seem so much more in earnest than they do amid the quiet villages of home."

About the middle of September the regiment was ordered to take position further up the river, on the Maryland shore. After marching three days, bivouacking at Darnstown and Poolesville, the Nineteenth came to a pleasant resting-place at Camp Benton, near Poolesville, and remained there until December.

CAMP BENTON.

Military life at this post is vividly depicted in our hero's letters, from which extracts will be given. From the following letter it appears that Newcomb was soon detailed as clerk at the Head-quarters of Brigadier-General F. W. Lander.

BRIGADE HEAD-QUARTERS,
CAMP BENTON, 23 SEPT., 1861.

DEAR BROTHER:

I will try to write you a few lines, though my fingers are so stiff I can hardly handle a pen. Last night I slept on a board floor, alone in a large tent, and as we had a little frost, this morning finds me cold and stiff. Two weeks ago today, I wrote to Col. Hinks. * * * Last Tuesday as I was washing my plate after dinner, I was summoned to his quarters. With fear and trembling, expecting some reprimand for crimes against I know not what, I obeyed. He questioned me as to my clerical ability, and under escort of a Lieutenant, sent me to Brigade Head-quarters; and I am for the present head-clerk to Brigadier-General F. W. Lander. Two have tried as assistants and been rejected. Manning was recommended and is now at work with me. The work is not so difficult but confining. Yesterday, for instance, when I expected a rest we were kept at work all day. It seems to be decreed to me—1st, that I shall not fight; 2nd, that I shall keep books and write. I value the position not so much for its intrinsic value as what it will bring. My health is excellent, and I find that the work which once excited me till nervousness and fever overcame all ability to work, now affects me little if any. Friday I received five letters. * * Thank the senders personally for me. The Adjutant went to Washington Saturday, and will probably return with my box. Please send no more boxes "till further orders." Enclosed I send a Countersign as it was sent us from Division Head-quarters, and was sent by us to each Reg't in the Brigade. In regard to your going to war, let me tell you that my office drill was of no use except as making me familiar with handling a gun; and that, as I would never have entered the ranks except in expectation of promotion, and could not carry my knapsack all the way on the first day's march, I could not advise you to enter, whose age, if nothing else, renders immediate promotion impossible, and whose strength and endurance are so soon at an end. So be content with selling pork and flour and collecting bills, and you cannot, in my opinion, find any situation either so pleasant or so conducive to health.

Last Tuesday night a mounted officer rode up to Head-quarters, and after private conversation with the General, rode off. Soon four companies of the 19th, this time not including Co. F, marched to Edwards Ferry or thereabouts. In expectation of an attempt on the part of the rebels to cross the river, they were posted in ambush and so lay all night. But there was no demonstration, and in the morning they returned. Saturday night four companies of the 19th again turned out. Manning went with them, but I who slept in the office at some little distance from the Reg't, was not awakened by their departure. Again the midnight march proved fruitless, except as showing the bravery of our soldiers. Without exception, the rank and file were most eager to fight, and those who were detailed for guard duty at the camp, in some instances offered money to comrades to change places with them, but these offers were refused. * * I have not been so well for years before. Direct letters to Brigade Head-quarters, Camp Benton, Md. Your Brother,

EDGAR.

The following descriptive paragraph is from a letter written by Knights on Oct. 2: From the hill in the rear of our lines the prospect is very fine. The regimental bands and the drums of the various corps at camp hours make noise enough, and the united sounds come up from the valley and re-echo among the encircling woods most wonderfully and beautifully. The morning landscape is especially charming; the ground itself and the white tents glittering with silver dew-drops; and the changing leaves of the gum tree and dogwood in the edge of the forest shining like burnished gold.

We are next favored with a glimpse of tent-life from Newcomb's facile pen.

BRIGADE HEAD-QUARTERS,
CAMP BENTON, OCT. 10, 1861.

DEAR BROTHER,

Not feeling fit for anything on account of a severe cold, I thought that the pleasantest use of some spare time would be to write my most frequent correspondent, excepting always our little Mother. The last letters I received were from Leila and Miss. P. After a first reading I treated them as I do all others—laid them aside for a second reading, after the fashion of the ruminants with their food. And as this suggests the matter of our rations, let me inform you that they are much better than formerly; yet even now we are at times reduced to hard bread and tea or coffee. Since I have "signed off" from these two last, bread and water do me for six hours at a time. Again at times we "feed" on beefsteak, potatoes and beans twice a day.

It is now growing quite cold and frosty for several nights at a time. Then comes a pouring rain-storm of two or three days, followed by a bitter cold wind. Having, after repeated colds and chills, become disgusted with sleeping on the ground, Manning (now my only tent-companion) and myself projected a bed. Two tent-poles, resting on rocks till they were raised 18 inches from the ground, formed the sides; several boards (begged, bought or stolen, according to the necessities of the case) formed the slats, and one huge log the pillow. Two ticks filled with straw, and confined within their proper limits by stakes driven alongside the bed, are our feathers. Having completed this yesterday, we retired early last night to enjoy it. But as I was unused to such luxuries, having slept on boards or the ground for two months, my sleep was light and interrupted. Tonight I hope to sleep better. From side to side of our tent, and half filling it, extends the double bed. From the ridge-pole are suspended our two rifles. Our candelabra is a horizontal slip of wood nailed to one of the "uprights." An old cracker box forms our secretary, and our harness is under the bed. We felt so much elated as we surveyed our domestic arrangements, that we have bought a box of blacking and blacking-brush. Tomorrow we may buy a looking-glass.

I was much pleased to learn that you are now contented to stay at home. I have met Prof. Schmitt, Captain of Co. E, 20th Reg., and several of my classmates. At first I was ashamed to speak to them. Of late I have gathered courage. I am the only one of all my acquaintances who has entered the ranks, and glorious as it will all be after promotion, the glory has not yet been revealed.

EDGAR.

The next letter reveals one of the mysteries of army cooking.

BRIGADE HD. QRS.,
CAMP BENTON, OCT. 11, 1861.

DEAREST SISTER:

Since writing to Charlie I have received Mother's two letters of Oct. 7 and 8; had a supper of hard bread and water, a night's rest on my new bed, to which I am becoming accustomed, and a breakfast of beans and hard bread. One article of diet I forgot to mention— "loosconce," a hash of hard bread and pork, boiled with water till it has acquired the consistency of chowder. It is not so bad, but in my remarks on the excellency of various dishes, remember the proverb, " hunger is the best sauce." This lobsconce is a rare dish, being furnished only when we have a sufficiency of pork and hard bread, and nothing else—three occurrences of very infrequent conjunction.

Your letter was received not long ago, and I will now attempt to answer your questions. Touching the shirts I do not yet need them, but when I do you shall surely hear. My needle-book has been little used, as Uncle Sam's seamstresses use strong thread and plenty of it. The leaf you *sent preserves its scent.* I am very grateful for these evidences of your love. As you have heard before this, my rank is not a Lieutenant's, nor the pay, nor the baggage allowed, but, if I am able, it soon shall be.

I am sorry to hear of Mr. Stone's delicate health, though not less that he is considering the feasability of going out with a regiment as Chaplain. Relinquishing all domestic joys, his large congregation and $4000 a year, for the roughness of camp life. But he knows his own business best. His sermon (in extract) which I received last night, was so good that I almost repented sending mother the message I did, but the copying of so much must be a troublesome job, and the pleasure it gives me hardly a compensation. On the table beside me lies the Congregationalist of Oct. 4, sent to Manning. It looks like New England.

Hereafter I shall not write regularly. I have written Sunday, because then the time was my own, and my thoughts all turned homeward; but now I have as much leisure almost any other day. Sometimes therefore I shall write oftener than once a week; sometimes not so often. There are so many things which I have neither time, nor patience, nor space, nor inclination to write, that they must be dropped and forgotten. My love to all enquiring friends.

Your aff.	BROTHER ED.

BALL'S BLUFF AND EDWARD'S FERRY.

" Come hither ye gallant men, and tell
The story of the day that Baker fell.
Tell of the storm, the darkness and the night,
Ye watched and waited for the coming fight."

The disastrous affair at Ball's Bluff took place on October 21, 1861. A portion of the official report of Colonel Hinks is given below: "Learning that a column of our troops was crossing the Potomac on the 21st, at a point near the centre of Harrison's Island, I hastened thither. With the 19th regiment I proceeded to the island. I learned that Colonel Baker had been killed, and found everything in confusion, our column being entirely routed. I at once took command, arrested as far as possible the progress of the rout, restored order, and, to check the advance of the enemy who threatened to occupy the island, I sent the 19th Massachusetts regiment to the front. After the passage of my regiment, no re-enforcements crossed to the island. * * The companies of the 19th and 20th were greatly exhausted, having been constantly employed in intrenching, burying the dead, removing the wounded, and transporting the artillery to and from the island."

Correspondent Knights gives the following particulars in a Massachusetts paper: "At Edward's Ferry the sharpshooters and Co. K of 'ours,' under command of Major How of the 19th, successfully repulsed three rebel regiments after continual skirmishing for eighteen hours. General Lander was with them a portion of the time, and received a wound which has proved so severe as to interfere with the discharge of his Brigade duties. Colonel Hinks is acting Brigadier during his absence. It seems not improbable that the Colonel will substitute stars for the eagles on his shoulder-straps."

An accurate plan of the battle of Ball's Bluff has been drawn by a member of the 19th Mass. Vols., and is in the possession of another veteran of the same regiment, Mr. John L. Robinson of Boston.

Captain Stephen I. Newman of Cambridgeport, Mass., (formerly Principal Musician of the 19th regiment) writes as follows: "I have the impression that Newcomb was orderly to General Lander at the battle of Edward's Ferry — the continuation of Ball's Bluff — and, if my memory serves me right, was promoted by recommendation of Adjutant John C. Chadwick, endorsed by General Lander, and approved by Colonel Hinks." Edgar was informed of his promotion in November, and the event is briefly referred to in one of his letters. In a subsequent letter Captain Newman kindly gives the following additional information: "The 19th Mass. was not in action at the battle called Ball's Bluff, Va., —but during the battle portions of it held Conrad's Ferry, Harrison's Island and Edward's Ferry, to re-enforce any part of the field that would send for assistance, and to preserve communication with the field on Oct. 21, 22. Two companies (H and K,) under Major H. J. How, did cross at Edward's Ferry to Virginia, and skirmished all day (22d) with the enemy. It is there Corporals Newcomb and Manning were with Brigadier General Fred. Lander, when Lander received his death-wound. The Regimental Color has on it 'Edward's Ferry, Va.' Edward's Ferry was the first place that the regiment was under fire."

Newcomb's brief comments on the battle appear in the following letter:

BRIGADE H'D QR's.
CAMP BENTON, OCT. 31, 1861.

DEAREST SISTER:

Almost a week has passed since I last wrote home, and no change has been made in the location of our Brigade; but on the other hand it becomes daily more probable we shall winter here. Yet as our arrangements are greatly modified by the movements of the enemy, there is still a possibility of our spending New Year's in a warmer climate. You have heard of our shameful retreats from Ball's Bluff to Harrison's Island, from thence to the Maryland shore, and about the same time from Virginia across Edward's Ferry to Maryland again. Not a single instance of cowardice occurred, but this time the shame falls wholly on our leaders, who planned the expeditions. Gen. Lander was so disgusted as in the excitement of the moment to say that unless he considered our ultimate success doubtful, he would resign at once. Perhaps, probably, his words meant more than he intended, but the general opinion hereabouts is that this war will be a long one. This doesn't make so much difference to me personally as it did three months ago, for I grow daily in love with the workings of this system. As Corporal in Co. F, I saw the lowest and heaviest of the machinery; as clerk here I see the workings of the whole machine, and despite numerous flaws and frictions, the results of ignorance and want of time, I am yet most greatly pleased therewith. I had hoped to be at home Thanksgiving, but the uncertainty of our plans and my peculiar position will prevent; unless (what is highly improbable) I return on public business. I had hoped to see at least our enterprising Bro. Charlie, perhaps also yourself or Mother this week, as the papers advertised a trip to Washington and back for $12 50, and from Washington to Camp is only a short stage-ride. * * * The General and staff went to Washington Saturday. He to get well before assuming command of the Cumberland district; his staff to get promotions so as to go with him. If he cannot take this Brigade with him, I have seen my last of Gen. Lander. Col. Hinks commands the Brigade for the present, and being at his own H'd Qr's, almost always we have great liberty. For example, yesterday, P. M., Manning and I chartered two horses of U. S., and went horseback riding. We go to bed about 8½. or whenever we please, and I get up about 7½ A. M. This morning we breakfasted on beefsteak, bread, butter and molasses and cheese at 8½. This P. M. we hope to ride again. Our tent is the absent Adjutant's, board floor, double roof. A wide trough filled with straw is our bed, and in the unaccustomed situation of Commander of the Brigade, the Col. and his Adj. entrust the management of affairs to the clerks themselves, only inspecting and endorsing our work. We usually finish work about 11 A. M., and spend the remainder of the day as we please. The whole Brigade has now an hour's daily drill with knapsacks.

An officer called to see me a few days ago. It was Capt. Drake. Soon after leaving Boston as 2d Lieut. of the 12th, Senator Wilson sent him a Lieut's commission in the Regulars ; and his next step was to become Ass't Adj't General on Gen. Abercrombie's staff. He is most fortunate and deserving. I was greatly pleased with his visit. He treated me with the utmost kindness and consideration.

I am patiently awaiting the arrival of that package, having but one pair of thick stockings, and that thoroughly perforated. Then I fear the next storm, as my boots are of little value. Uncle Sam has both shoes and stockings, but he has little regard to *fitness*, and I want clothing from home. While we read of hot weather in New York and Boston, we often awake in the morning to find the fields as white as ½ hour's heavy snowing could make them, the dampness and frost are so great.

Your letters (polyglot and all) are duly received. Also three papers from Mother and one from Stanley. Mr. Stone sent me a note, for which I am most grateful. His sermon also, copied by Mother, was exceedingly interesting, the best essay of any kind I have read or heard for months.

The wounded of the Twentieth are all doing well. Capt. Schmitt has only the wounds of two balls, which passed completely through, instead of five as at first supposed. * * Give Ed. my best regards whenever you may direct a letter to him, for by this time I suppose he is on his way Southward.

EDGAR.

Even the dire confusion and indescribable anguish of battle may soon give place to the regular routine of camp-duty, and ere long our army friends write as though nothing had happened.

BRIGADE HEAD-QUARTERS,
CAMP BENTON, NOV. 6, 1861.

DEAR BROTHER:

My next letter was to have been directed to Mother, but the reception, day before yesterday, of your letter changed my intention, and little Mother must wait till next time. I rejoice at the prospect of good things to come (for our Lieut. with the box is not yet returned from Washington,) and I am grateful to you and the others with a gratitude which only the actual possession of your gifts can enchance. * * Tell S. that I laid aside all College lore and critical propensity with my civilian clothes at Lynnfield. He need therefore fear nothing worse than an answer at my earliest convenience. * * My reading matter is military books of which I have no lack. Anything else, except the papers you have so freely sent, would not *at present* be acceptable. Tracts are plenty at the Chaplain's quarters, but I could do nothing with them. Let me describe the persons and doings of several, for Father's edification. And first, Gen. Lander—a very tall spare man of a huge sinewy frame, a high retreating forehead and iron-gray hair. He rides a white horse whose foreshoulders are as high as my head. Few of the attaches of this establishment dared mount him. The General loves to be praised and petted, though not a man dares disobey him, and when roused his enemies had better slink away. He is very nervous and restless when there is no fighting.

The former Aide-de-Camp, whose autograph I send you, was on Butler's staff in "the three months" and covered the retreat at Big Bethel. He is only two days older than myself, very robust florid, talented and witty, a universal favorite, now Captain in the Regulars. Col. Hinks, now in command, is a most agreeable and soldier-like man, prepossessing at the first, and improving with acquaintance. * * Lieut. Dodge, after the fight at Ball's Bluff, crossed to Virginia with a flag of truce, to look after the dead. He approached within two or three miles of Leesburg, and performed his duty so bravely as to win the praise of the Colonel. Prentiss is now transferred to the commissary department. Colburn is sadly homesick. He is one of the eight corporals who guard the colors.

Of the four postage stamps Mother sent me, one I gave away, two paid for a pint of molasses, and the last found its way to Boston on my last letter. I am greatly rejoiced at your steadfast purpose to stay at home. All the family need you, and to my thinking it requires more courage to give up military reputation than to suffer the privations of camp-life. In fact the actual experience of this last is neither so terrible nor exciting, nor painful as the imagination paints it, and

bears to the imagination about the same relation as does a sea-faring
life.   EDGAR.

Newcomb's clerkship at Head-quarters terminated soon after
the last letter was written, and it also appears that he was ill
about this time.   Capt. W. E. Barrows, formerly Hospital Steward
of the 19th regiment, writes: "I am happy to say that Edgar's
friendship was enjoyed by me from the first.   I think I met him
first as a patient in the hospital at Poolesville—after he had left
General Lander's office."

After his promotion as Sergeant Major of the regiment,
our hero gives another graphic account of life under canvas.

CAMP BENTON, Nov. 15, 1861.

DEAR BROTHER:
    The day is rainy, my box is not yet arrived at camp, and since
mounting guard and finishing the Regimental morning report I have
had nothing to do but try to keep myself dry and warm—no easy job
when the soil is soft, and boots are full of holes, and smoke is the only
result of an hour's effort to build a fire.   Our apparatus for heating is
quite simple and primitive.   A trough about 18 inches deep and 2
feet wide is dug from the centre of the tent to the outside.   This is
covered with broad flat stones, a barrel over the outer end forms a
chimney, and the whole is plastered with mud.   A small opening left
in the centre of the tent serves as a door for the admission of fuel
and, when the winds are contrary, for the exit of smoke.   Over the
fire-place I am now seated, my feet warmed by the covering stones in
the Sergeant Major's tent, a room about 10 feet square.   My bed, my
seat, is a straw tick covered with my blankets and supported on tent-
poles, themselves resting on four uprights.   On the other side is the
bed of Quartermaster Sergeant Frank Briggs.   Both beds foot toward
the entrance.   Between and at their head stands our table, before it
a stationary stool, while from the ridge-pole depends a horizontal bar
whereon are hung our knapsacks, haversacks, canteens, sashes and my
sword.   This last descends to me hereditarily from the previous in-
cumbent.   This is my home, and I enjoy far better health and spirits
than in the shelter and comfort I have always experienced heretofore.
In all beside, relating to mind or body, the comparison fails.   Thus
one great purpose of my undertaking is successful beyond expectation.
    I have also noticed a vast improvement in the quantity and
quality of my "grub" since I began to mess with the non-commissioned staff.   But not a day passes that I do not long to be home for

a while. As Thanksgiving draws near, this desire increases, but most vainly. We too shall celebrate as we can, and in the evening I shall attend a ball to be given within the lines, if I am invited, but I shall not be at home. We intend to have a splendid time, and my next letter will give you the details. I am now called to form the line for dress parade, and after supper will continue.

FRIDAY EVENING.

You are probably on the way to evening meeting. Remember me there. Last Sunday I listened to the parting discourse of our Chaplain, and the second I had ever heard from him. Sunday eve I attended prayer-meeting at the 7th Mich. My friend of the Regiment left for his native State about a week ago. * * Hereafter direct letters, papers and packages, Sergeant Major, 19 Mass. Vols., Camp Benton, near Poolesville.

E. M. N.

Four Harvard graduates were at this time in the 19th Massachusetts — Major Henry Jackson How, class of 1859; Assistant Surgeon Josiah Newell Willard, class of 1857; Capt. George Wellington Batchelder, class of 1859; Sergeant Major Edgar Marshall Newcomb, class of 1860. On one occasion, at least, as we learn from Correspondent Knights, the delightful melody of "Fair Harvard" was played by the band. "We, the Colonel and staff, have been serenaded by the band, and as the parting cadence of 'Fair Harvard' died away beneath the moonlight, I must confess that tears would come to my eyes; nor could I force them back, even at the ringing strains of the 'Star Spangled Banner.'"

THANKSGIVING DAY IN CAMP.

The observance of this festival at Camp Benton is described by Newcomb in the following extract from a letter written to his father on Nov. 23, 1861:

The programme for the day was excellent, but ill-performed. The dining and dancing hall, which should have been finished the night before, was not ready till 5 P. M. of the 21st. Therefore the exhibitions intended to amuse the men were postponed. However, the officers and invited guests to the number of one hundred sat down to dinner. With my usual fortune I arrived as the last seat was taken, and when at last room had been made and I flourished my knife over turkey and potatoes preparatory to dining, Col. Hinks arose to speak, and of course all gustatory exercises was at an end. With becoming patience I waited till toasts and speeches were ended and the assembly dismissed. But the victuals were stone cold and a violent colic followed. In the evening we had a ball. The ladies invited from Baltimore were beautiful, the music excellent; but a friend delivering me letters from Charles, Leila and Mother, I bolted incontinently from the room to "my home." 'Twas my Thanksgiving dinner indeed, and let no one, even my constant brother Charlie, think for a moment that letters any rarer or shorter could be pleasanter.

About 2 next A. M. the assembly dissolved, not a few the worse for champagne and sherry, which flowed like water all the afternoon and evening. Next day we formed a hollow square to witness the climbing of a greased pole after $5. Many were the aspirants, but ten feet was the utmost limit of their skill and endurance. Next followed a race in bags, where the racer was not even permitted the use of his arms. The experiment was most successful in raising the laughter of the crowd, as the poor contestants hopped and fell and rolled helplessly in the inexorable "gunnies." A foot-ball game between the two wings of the Reg't was projected but not executed.

The wagon which conveyed some of our guests to Adamstown returned last evening after I had retired, and the pattering rain warning me of wet feet on the morrow made me think of the box. In the morning I hastened out, and to my joyful surprise received it, four weeks less two days after it left home. I was most grateful for the numberless gifts and delicacies your care had provided. Only one apple was spoiled. The boots were all I could wish as to size and quality. Manning and myself were duly thankful for the pistols, so exquisite the workmanship, so delicate the bore, so light yet so tasteful; with the sermons, pamphlets and notes from Mother, Leila and Charles. The India rubbers I wore at guard-mounting, the calfskins I now have on, as well as the glazing which protects a cap once dark blue, now pale red with exposure to snow and rain.

I have received part of my pay, and will forward it by a friend in a few days. I expect the rest daily, but the Lieutenant's pay I was told accrued to my clerkship has dwindled from $100 to ¼ that sum. It makes no difference to me so long as I have more than enough, but I am only sorry to have raised false expectations by premature information. It is yet uncertain, though improbable, that we go into winter quarters. I should laugh if Ed. Hall were confined for the next few months to a fortress, and the 19th sent into Secessia, conquering and to conquer. Tell Mother not to fear for my safety, for my position in line of battle is not as before in the front rank, but eight paces in rear of the file-closers on the extreme left. * * Let everything be paid for out of my wages, remembering how you would prize the feeling of independence yourself.

While I write, the drums are beating the dead-march to the playing of the band. Another, and the third since we came to Camp Benton, is carried to his last home, away from kindred, deprived of even a religious service, for the Chaplain is away. His company follow him to the grave, he is lowered to the rolling of muffled drums, earth falls on the coffin as eight comrades and a corporal fire three volleys over the grave,—and then leave him for the bright carelessness of life again. It sickens me to live in such an atmosphere. Man lives and dies like a brute. And now the company is marching back to the tune of "Yankee Doodle," and a son of Erin chopping wood before the tent-door remarks, "That fellow is in his grave." We are summoned to Dress Parade, and informing you that Capt. Schmitt and Lieut. Lowell are at home on furloughs, I bid you good bye.

EDGAR.

The name of the deceased soldier was John Fitzgerald. By referring to the record of a similar event which occurred about six months later, it will be seen that Newcomb's reflections on the military funeral were not in vain.

Correspondent Knights describes the Thanksgiving festival as follows :

Nov. 23, 1861.

Of all the anomalies in this war for the flag, none appears so striking as the recent celebration of our annual Thanksgiving. Reveille was beat amid the firing of a national salute by the batteries of the Brigade; the bands afterwards performing at Head-quarters, accompanied by salvos of artillery. The boys had an appetite for the dinner of turkey and fixings generously provided for them. They had been watching anxiously the flock of one hundred and fifty gobblers which had been fattening in the field for some days; and to these were added as many more from private sources. A military concert and ball in the evening was the grand affair of the day. Carpenters and sail-makers had erected in front of Head-quarters a pavilion forty feet by thirty-five, with retiring rooms and a refreshment saloon attached. The fair guests who graced the assembly were invited, and came, to the number of forty from Baltimore—a distance of seventy-five miles. After such a proof of loyalty, it would certainly be unjust to say that the Baltimore belles are not for the Union. "Taps" were suspended by special order, and it was not until first cock-crowing that the camp was still. Thanksgiving Day of the year of our Lord, 1861, had been in the camp of the Nineteenth Regiment, Mass. Vols., an eminently gay and festive occasion. But who of us would dare look forward to another such as this?

CAMP BENTON,
MONDAY EVE., NOV. 25, 1861.

DEAREST SISTER:

After an almost perfect rest of two weeks, in the necessary absence of drill before Thanksgiving, I am somewhat tired tonight from an afternoon drill of 2½ hours. Last night we had the first snow-storm of the season: nothing severe, however. The spare time of today has been spent in greasing boots, oiling gun, and sewing on buttons, of which I am now in need. * * And now as to the box. The boots fit so well that before Sunday night I had worn holes in each stocking, and now my feet are sore. Of the eatables, none can I at present eat, except the crackers: though everything has been tasted. Apples and soft crackers cannot be found here. Sardines, however, are plenty at 25 and 50 cents per box. The bundle has not yet arrived. As my two blankets proved insufficient protection after leaving Manning, the Adjutant furnished me with a comforter the ladies of Salem had sent to suffering volunteers, and every night I bless those ladies, as I enjoy their gift.

You especially, though all the family more generally, must feel lonesome that the little Lieut. has gone, and I greatly wish I were with you to comfort and cheer you now. Yet how fortunate that, instead of a sudden and hurried departure, you were permitted to be gradually weaned, as it were, that the great burden of separation might gradually fall upon you. Somehow as I think of you all, I cannot feel lonely, though associating familiarly with not a man in the camp, except him whose occasional visits are brief and hurried. I enjoy imaging you around the table, or the fire, or the family altar, and I am never lonely. To you matters are different. You can never tell how we are situated, or where we are, but yet somewhat of that same fancy which so blesses me in leisure moments cannot but amuse you, if you will abstract yourself from home and self. But a higher and holier joy lies in this—that we are children of a common Father, and each engaged in his Father's business, though in different apartments of the same home. The harmony in our thoughts, and feelings, and purposes, and affections, is a bond which is stronger than separation, or distance, or life itself.

I have done up my Algebra as a present for Charlie; the shoes in which I did all my marching and drilling as a Corporal; and stockings which with the shoes were on the march up the river, and on Harrison's Island the night of Oct. 21st. My love to all.

EDGAR.

P. S. Your letters was the most grateful and beneficial of all the contents of the box.

Next come portions of letters (including a poem) from Correspondent Knights. The first is written shortly before leaving Camp Benton.

CAMP BENTON, DEC. 3.

The 19th Massachusetts has gained a reputation hereabouts for almost every military virtue, and it is a matter of great pride to us, of course. I found, too, while at home, that to be one of the 19th was an "open sesame" to every circle. We have received marching orders. The regiment will move tomorrow morning at eight o'clock, via Edwards Ferry and canal boat to Seneca Mills. "The line of the Potomac, from Great Falls to Seneca Mills (14 miles) is to be entrusted to the guard of the 19 Reg't, Mass. Vols., Col. E. W. Hinks." So reads the order.

CAMP NEAR MUDDY BRANCH, SENECA, MD.

DEC. 9, 1861.

Camp Benton is no longer "ours." We left it a monument, so long as its landmarks shall remain, of the military genius, the ingenuity and perseverance of the officers and men of the Mass. 19th. Its well-determined lines, its spacious streets, its curiously-constructed ovens and underground furnaces, its nicely-thatched stables and log-houses—all bear testimony to the versatile skill of the men of the Old Bay State. We are hardly established in our new quarters. The Colonel has his Head-quarters in an old but not inconvenient house, where we manage to make ourselves comfortable in this vicinage of mist and malaria. The three companies on picket, the details for extra duty as wood-choppers and builders in the construction of the block-houses, and the necessary quarters-guard exhaust all of the effective force in the regiment.

Just in front of our lines, on the crest of the undulating swells that diversify the face of this section, at the foot of a cluster of spruce trees, that shade it from the glow of the hot noon-time, is an enclosure, and within its rustic fence lately lay the remains of Oliver Younger, Jr., 12th Mass. Vols. The ground is still occupied by another member of the same regiment. Their bodies rested side by side. Yesterday was most delightful, almost a summer's day, and as I stood at the color-line, looking in that direction, the little burial ground in the midst of the camp suggested the following:

YONDER IS HEAVEN.

Under the shadow of a clump of spruces,
  A rustic paling doth the spot enclose,
Where, worn and weary with life's various uses,
  Two tired soldiers in their rest repose.

The moss-grown branches, to the skies upreaching
  Their weird bare arms all desolate and gray,
Seem ever to the soul this lesson teaching:
  "Yonder is heaven; yonder, too, the way."

Yonder is found no panoply of battle,
  No brilliant trappings and no gleaming steel,
No war of cannon and no muskets' rattle,
  No tramp of horsemen and no rumbling wheel.

Yonder is heard no watcher's sad entreating,
  There is no sob, or tear, or mourner's cry;
On yonder plains no gallant heart is beating,
  Longing to live, yet praying still to die.

Yonder is Peace! The setting sunlight glancing
  Athwart the slabs with gold and crimson ray,
Inscribed thereon, in words of light entrancing:
  "Yonder is Heaven—This is but the way."

The new camp was situated near Muddy Branch, in the vicinity of Seneca, Md., and not far from the Potomac. In the following letters interesting particulars are given. It will be noticed that our gallant soldier refuses to accept "defensive armor."

CAMP NEAR MUDDY BRANCH,
DEC. 15, 1861.

DEAR BROTHER:
  Since last Sunday I have received letters from yourself, Father, Mother, Stanley and Gilbert Webber. While I thank you for your

kind interest for my comfort and safety, I decline all kinds of defensive armor as useless and cumbersome. I do not yet feel destined to a violent death in this war, but if you wish to spend 8 dollars on my account, give them to the Bible Society. My tent is pitched, though yet unoccupied. I am waiting for a stove which I expect tomorrow. Meanwhile I sleep on the floor of head-quarters, but I hope this night is the last, as I wish to be alone in "my home." Around the edges are laid logs to keep out the wind, and logs in two tiers form a pen which I have filled with hay for a bed. * * Our regiment was increased day before yesterday by 122 recruits from Mass., commanded by Capt. C. U. Devereux, brother of our Lieut. Col. His men are fine-looking, but appear most ludicrously raw to us veterans of four months. As a natural concomitant they think themselves "some sojer," and have a way of expostulating when they believe themselves right, which is strange to us who know nothing but our orders. A few nights ago Manning came from an old camp, and spent the night with me. He is still engaged as clerk at Brigade Head-quarters. We have no drills now, as 8-10 of our men are on picket at the river, and off cutting timber for our log houses. The Colonel has sent for his family and doesn't expect to march before February next. Every Sabbath I wish I were at home. However, those now spent are far pleasanter than previous ones. * * Those who have returned to us from furloughs declare themselves glad to return to their work here, matters at home were so dull. Now good-night.

EDGAR.

CAMP NEAR MUDDY BRANCH.
DEC. 22, 1861.

DEAR BROTHER:

This letter will be mailed tomorrow, so as to arrive home Christmas. Please consider it a present—as all I can give now. My own presence I must bestow elsewhere. For months to come, both duty and interest will probably require me to be in the camp of the 19th. * * Today there has been no religious service except the prayer on dress parade, and this afternoon I found time to go to the river, about ten minutes walk from here. Our pickets extend for twelve miles along the canal, their mud huts being clearly visible from the Virginia side of the river. Looking over into Secessia one sees only the ordinary landscape of hill and dale and forest, interspersed with houses and cattle—not the least sign of war. A stranger here would never suspect the presence of a body of soldiers, much less of two armies. Our block houses, three in number, are to occupy as many bluffs, each commanding long reaches of the river and country on either side.

We all long for an opportunity to cross, and so surely as Mc'Call's Division, only seven miles below us on the Virginia shore, succeeds in driving the rebels further up, we march to hold the conquest. At present, however, I am not in good marching order, my new boots had worn the skin from a small place on the inside of the right ankle before we left Camp Benton. On the march I wore the new boots. The sore festered, and not till yesterday was I able to wear them again. Weeks will perhaps pass before my lameness is at an end. * * The weather here is chilly but pleasant. We have had no rain for two weeks. My tent is warmed by a stove of sheet iron, costing me the sum of $2.50. Tell Father, Mr. Prentiss is now Quartermaster Sergeant. I mess wtth him daily, and no one in camp lives better than we. It is now supper time—enough for the present.

Supper is ended, my work for the day finished, and I may devote the evening to reading and writing. The amount of my business may be imagined when it is known that I have not yet had time to read the Harper's you sent me, or the book on rifles. The business is quite varying from day to day, and uncertain in its extent. Now I have half a day to myself, besides plenty of time for exercise; again, I am occupied the whole day and into the night. It has begun to rain with a good prospect of three or four days' continuance.

Hoping this may arrive in time to make your dinner relish better, and wishing you all a most Merry Christmas, I must close. I shall enjoy myself on that day not less, perhaps, than last year.

EDGAR.

Correspondent Knights briefly describes the situation on Christmas, 1861.

CAMP NEAR MUDDY BRANCH, MD.

DEC. 25, 1861.

Christmas in camp! It has its merry times, though there be no Santa Claus to pop into its tape-tied tent-doors, and down its sooty stove-pipes. So far as the weather goes, nature has favored our Christmas time exceedingly. The dismal, drizzly rain of the last day or two has given place to a clear, bracing atmosphere, which reminds us of New England Octobers. The night air is chill, and the teeth of the shivering sentry chatter as he walks his beat; but the sun comes up from behind the pines and streams, with a certain warmth, before I hear the drums at "orderly hour" along the color line; and the Corporal calls us with a "Merry Christmas, gentlemen."

A NEW YEAR'S LETTER FROM CAMP.

CAMP NEAR SENECA,

JAN. 1, 1862.

DEAREST SISTER:

For several days I have been seeking an opportunity to write home, but the business of the closing year has prevented it till now. * * The eatables are not yet all gone. One piece of mince-pie remains. Apples, chocolate, jelly and nuts are not half devoured. Don't send another box by express, for I am fully provided with every thing needful. The Colonel's wife and child, with whom he goes home in about two weeks, are to stop at our Hd. Qrs. I have not yet been introduced, though I see Mrs. Hinks almost daily.

Yesterday I went to Poolesville on some law business for Alonzo Alden, riding in all 30 miles in a team without springs, and over execrable roads. I was unsuccessful in finding the party, and moreover, was left by the teams, and walked over 2 miles before I overtook them. At 9 P. M. our mess had a supper, at which the Colonel and his staff were present, and all manner of luxuries including egg-nog and lemonade-punch. graced the board. Though I havn't lost confidence in my own will, yet I have often felt (not thought only) that the total abstinence pledge has a worth to myself unappreciated before, and were it not for this I could hardly resist the temptations to imbibe most palateable concoctions of liquors on our frequent "special occasions."

You are doubtless curious to know about our mess. It consists of eleven. The cooking is done by a professed cook, and superintended by Prentiss. We have flap-jacks, butter and molasses, with beefsteak or chickens, sometimes pie or rice for dinner. This is the usual bill of fare, but so varied that every thing tastes good. Nor do we pay anything but what is made up to us by surplus rations. Coffee and tea were my daily drink in Co. F, but when I was taken from active to sedentary life I found they injured me. Supper is ready. Farewell.

8 P. M.

Beefsteak, potatoes and toast. The weather today has been exceedingly warm. The night comes on with a mighty wind, which in my absence scattered the papers upon the floor. Thus do I account for divers spots looking like tobacco-juice, but which are only Maryland alluvium. Every cord of the tent is strained, and the clattering and flutter is as great in proportion as that of the "Admiral" in a storm at sea. The wind blows my candle, joggles my desk, and makes such a noise I can hardly think. Gen. Lander in a couple of weeks will go up the river. Manning goes with the General. I am sorry we are to be separated, but it is best in some way. I have heard of Ed. Hall's final settlement on that clump of sand, Ship Island, and grateful am I that I am not there with him, with such imperfect means of enjoyment and communication with home. However, he will not remain there long, and his happy disposition will triumph over the sand heap and the muddy brine. * * I hear there has been some talk of visiting me. Our camp is only a few minutes distant from the Ohio and Chesapeake Canal, Muddy Branch Lock. You can also come by stage from Washington to Darnestown, and a team which brings the mail daily from that place to camp will also carry you. But if any of you are coming to see me, let me know both the time and way of your coming, that I may find you, which will be far easier than your finding me. * * I hope you never feel lonely and sad. We who have given up all never feel so, and you who have so much left should be very happy. The present is cheerful enough, while the good time coming, not far distant let us hope, will be how much happier than now. I was never happier in my life (and the more you think of it the stranger it will seem). Why then should anybody be less happy than myself? It is as much our duty as our privilege to enjoy ourselves; and in this duty, if in no other, obedience brings its own reward.

Capt. Rice is soon to go home on a furlough, and Lieut. Rice with several others of our Regiment are ordered home on recruiting service. You see how long a letter I have sent you, and it would be longer under different circumstances. Now when you answer, don't stint yourself to filling out a small sheet of note paper, but give me enough to feed on for a while.

Brother,   EDGAR.

Mr. John L. Robinson has kindly allowed an artist-friend, Mr. F. H. C. Woolley, to make a sketch from the original photograph of the " Camp near Muddy Branch." Only a small portion of the camp is represented, and the artist has not attempted to re-produce all the soldiers who appear in the photograph. Sergeant Major Newcomb holds a paper which is the morning report of the regiment. His features do not appear distinctly.

CAMP NEAR SENECA,
JAN. 19, 1862.

DEAR MOTHER:

Allow me to introduce Mr. Bishop, First Lieutenant of the Tiger Zouaves of our regiment—the bearer of this note and of two photographs of our Head-quarters. A description may not be uninteresting.

Beginning on the right: the two small tents contain our ammunition; the wall-tents are the Quartermaster's; the bell-tent contains clothing, as also do the boxes before it. The house has four rooms—an office and reception room below; a store room and chamber for the Colonel and wife above. Figure No. 1 is Knights, clerk at Head-quarters; No. 2, Adjutant Reynolds; 3, Lieut. Bishop, then Officer of the Day; 4, clerk with Quarter-master; 5, Prentiss, Quarter-master Sergeant; 6, Dr. Dyer, Surgeon; 7, Quarter-master Shaw; 8, an Orderly Sergeant; 9, clerk; 10, sentry; 11, Sergeant Major with Morning Report book. The remainder are Head-quarters servants or sentries, till on the extreme left, with drawn sword Lieut. White of a detachment of Cavalry stationed here. His horse is dimly seen: owing not so much to the quality of government oats, as to the restlessness of the animal. In a few days I will write again.

Your loving Son,   EDGAR.

Received since last letter home letters from yourself, Charlie and Sister. Papers from yourself and Charlie and Stanley.

At the close of the following letter, and also in other communications, Edgar refers to his mother's unpleasant dreams concerning her soldier-boy. Were these visions providential forewarnings of coming sorrow?

CAMP NEAR SENECA,
JAN. 21, 1862.

DEAR BROTHER:

Yesterday I sent home by Lt. Bishop "of ours" a couple of photographs of our Head-quarters. The establishment of the artist was on these grounds when we first came, though the artist himself was absent. I did not know of his return till I saw him behind his instrument on the day he took the aforesaid impression. Therefore I omitted getting a nearer view of his machine. He left here the next day; therefore I was unable to sit afterward. A magnifying glass will disclose the features of the persons more perfectly, and a key may be made by tracing the figures in transparent paper, numbering and naming them. If a convenient opportunity offers I shall send home my gun and equipments. The gun is taken to pieces and boxed up with cartridge-box, cap-box, &c. Though your curiosity may be strong to see the gun put together, my own preference is that it remain as you receive it till my return. Tell Mother that I don't *at present* wish her or any of the family to visit me; but if she should raise the curtain of my tent, her welcome would be hearty enough to give her complete satisfaction. I am sorry Mother's dreams of me are so frequently unpleasant.

In the next letter, which contains not a trace of empty boasting, the Sergeant Major artlessly confesses that his impetuous spirit was aroused by the echoes of a distant conflict, and he was eager to take part in the action. The brave warrior is always thus inspired by the music of the guns.

WEDNESDAY EVENING, JAN. 22.

After a sumptuous supper of fried and baked fresh haddock, I sit down to write you. A fire is roaring in the stove, and everything is as cheerful as can well be in our canvas dormitory. I begin with thanking Stanley for the confectionery he sent me so long ago. I think the fisheries must have been generally unsuccessful, there occurred so many imitation codfish in my two pounds of candy. * * The weather which for the last week has been manifest in constant rain, reducing the ground in the vicinity of my tent to a mortar-bed, strove to clear up matters last night by a snowstorm, but ineffectually. Today there have been attempts at a gale. In vain; the clouds will not break up their meeting.

Almost every day, certainly every third day, we hear the distant roar of cannon, and of musketry. Oh, how nervous it makes me to listen, as I did three days ago, to the continuous discharge of cannon and rifles for hours, and know that there was fighting there. Such are the only times I am impatient to go forward. I took the opportunity not long ago to call on the Chaplain, and two hours were passed very pleasantly in religious discourse. Several hours a day can now be devoted to reading, and the small library at Head-quarters furnishes matter for thought. My visitors laugh at my library, consisting of three books—"Holy Bible" between "Infantry Tactics" and "Army Regulations." Good night.

EDGAR.

CAMP NEAR SENECA,
JAN. 24, 1862.

DEAREST SISTER:

Know that I have conscientious scruples against writing home more frequently than once a week. My time is too valuable; my leisure too small for such light employment. But a letter from Charlie received tonight, in which he mentions that folks at home are dolorously affected in view of my change of residence, inclined me to write,

and as I betook myself to the task the unexpected sight of my own
initials, stamped on this sheet by your own affectionate love, fully decided me. The stamp was one I had not noticed before, and it is
grateful as beautiful.

First then, as to going to Ship Island. A week ago the rumor
first reached us that Col. Hinks, promoted to Brig. Gen., was to take
the 15th, 19th and 20th Mass. and 7th Mich. Regt's to Ship Island.
At once imagination transferred the scene of the severest struggles
and brightest victories to the mouth of the Mississippi. We were not
to go to Annapolis, however, for embarkation before Feb. 1. Under
these circumstances I wrote my last. But though this time rumor
started from Hd. Qrs., it was baseless as ever; the bubble exploded,
and today its place is supplied by a fresher one, namely: We are soon
to go across the Potomac. The roar of McCall's cannon daily grows
louder, and from the hill-tops we have seen their smoke ; and at the
same time long trains of wagons disappearing behind the distant hills,
as the rebels move southward before them. As you know, I could
not now obtain leave of absence even for a week. Col. Hinks soon
returns to lead his Reg't (not his Brigade.) and we hope to acquire
other laurels than for making a good retreat from Harrison's Island
and building block-houses on Maryland bluffs. Tonight while I write,
not two miles from the Virginia shore, a body of 500 determined men
could cross, capture officers, men, ammunition and Quartermaster's
stores, and make good their escape with their booty; for we are the
only Reg't on this side within ten miles, and scattered all along the
river-bank. But Secesh either don't know our helplessness, or don't
care to make the dash at us—probably the latter. I must end this
letter and betake myself to Morning Report and Guard Detail; and,
after work, to Plutarch whose "Lives" I am trying to digest. Good
Night. Is that word as sweet to hear from me as ever ?

EDGAR.

In February, 1862, Newcomb was agreeably disappointed by
receiving permission to return home on a short furlough. The joy
with which he was greeted by relatives and friends cannot be expressed in words. With a single exception it was the last time
that any of them saw him alive. His cordial greeting and noble
bearing can never be forgotten. At this time he was the picture
of health. On parting with him then, some of us could not
believe that it was for the last time on earth.

Soon after returning to military duty he writes as follows:

CAMP NEAR SENECA,
MARCH 3, 1862.

DEAR SISTER:

Since my last letter I have received letters from Mother and yourself up to Feb. 28. I would have written yesterday, but part of the day was occupied in moving our tents to a healthier situation. As you know, all of Banks' and Sedgewick's (formerly Stone's) Divisions, except our Brigade, have crossed the river, and perhaps before my next, we too shall tread the ——— soil, but as yet we have no marching orders.

One of the strange experiences of my life occurred day before yesterday. Our field officers had a few hours before received swords which an uncle of Lieut. Dodge had imported from France. As I was standing at Hd. Qrs. the gentleman entered and was introduced to the officers. I remembered at once having seen him before, and in a pause of the conversation asked him if I had not met him in Paris. "Bless me, yes," said he, and rising shook my hand most heartily. He proved to be Mr. Clark, the clerk of the American ex-Minister at Paris, who so interested himself in me, and wrote me once or twice after my return. As a traveller I parted from him in Paris a little more than 18 months ago, one bright autumn afternoon ; and to meet him again as a soldier on the Potomac at military Hd. Qrs., about the same hour of a gusty winter's day. Yesterday we parted, and he promised another rendezvous at Richmond. * * * I never had an experience which in memory seemed more like a dream than my visit home, and never parted from friends (myself to leave them) when the farewell was to me so sad and painful. I do not think I shall be many months out of the way if I prophesy that I shall spend next New Year's day at home.

EDGAR.

I re-open this letter to mention the reception of Mother's letter with Jamie's flag—a splendid triumph—and newspapers, Advertiser, Journal and Congregationalist.

Perhaps Edgar's prophesy was fulfilled in a very true sense.

———————

FAREWELL TO MUDDY BRANCH.

CAMP NEAR SENECA,
MCH. 8, 1862.

DEAR BROTHER:

Here we still lie in the mud, though your papers have it that we have crossed the river. Never since I enlisted have I felt so impatient to move. We hear that all the armies of the north are moving, except that alone which has suffered the sorest defeats and is most eager to avenge them. At Big Bethel, Bull Run and Ball's Bluff, the army on the banks of the Potomac have been worsted without the compensation of a single victory of importance. In addition, Banks' Division have all crossed, and every Brigade in our Division but ours. General Lander has died of his wounds received long ago, and yesterday Col. Hinks sent for Manning to return to his company. If he returns he will experience a great vicissitude of fortune, having fallen at once from his easy office-life, the society of officers and gentlemen, and the prospect of immediate promotion to Lander's staff,—down to the simple fare and brutal society and hard usage of a Corporal. I heartily sympathize with him and hope it may not be so. During the past week we have raised an immense tent, some sixty feet square, and the Chaplain projects great and varied amusements which I hope may be realized. To-morrow we shall probably hold our first service there. A few days ago the non-commissioned officers of the Regiment received their warrants. I will forward mine as soon as possible, which may not be for many weeks. Manning wrote me that the carpenter whom he had hired to make the box for my gun and equipments made it too small, and the Quartermaster forbade his making another. So my treasure which I had supposed long ago boxed up and ready for shipment, remains as it was the day of my promotion. It is to be forwarded to Camp at some future day, and before the war is ended it will probably be at home. Thus far only can I promise.

Rumor is at last true. The order from Head-quarters has come, that we hold ourselves in readiness to move at the shortest notice. Probably before next Wednesday, possibly to-morrow, we are to bid good-bye to " Camp near Muddy Branch."

EDGAR.

The marches of the Nineteenth Mass., from the time of leaving Muddy Branch until the regiment took cars for Washington, are recorded in Newcomb's letter dated March 30, 1862.

AT WASHINGTON AGAIN.

WASHINGTON, MARCH 26, '62.

DEAR LEILA:

We arrived in Washington yesterday, and rumor has it that to-day we leave this place to go into camp at Alexandria for the present. You may write me letters up to the last of this month with a good chance of my receiving them. I spent my last cent this morning for breakfast, and the Regiment is played out as regards money, so that I shall probably be unable to borrow any, and for the present must live on Uncle Sam alone. We are stopping in the same building where we stopped last August. The lodging is however, inside instead of outside the building, and our living vastly superior to what it was before. The bread is fresh, but the coffee is of doubtful purity, and the cold tongue of undoubted age.

I received five letters on the day after mailing my last — from Mother, yourself, Charlie, Gilbert and Deacon Hoyt; also a short note from James, besides Congregationalist, Gazette, &c. My trunk was left behind in the storehouse of the 19th, at Harper's Ferry. The details of our march from Muddy Branch till our arrival at our destination, whatever that may be, will be given as soon as I can find leisure and comfort.

Mother is probably this morning in Troy, comforting poor Grandfather, and you are the mistress of the household.

The delays to which we are everywhere subject, whenever we are to ride instead of march, are the most vexatious things of a soldier's experience. Long before this we might have arrived where it is designed to send us, if contractors &c. were half as earnest in their work as the men.

But good-bye and love to all.   Affectionately,

                                                        EDDIE.

ON THE POTOMAC. DESTINATION UNKNOWN.

SUNDAY EVENING, MCH. 30, 1862.

ON THE POTOMAC.

DEAR BROTHER:

The time which for the present I call my own I devote to writing home; but a steamer crowded with 900 souls, and a small cabin overflowing with shoulder-straps, are not conducive to concentration or continuity of thought. Ever since a week ago next Tuesday we have travelled hither and thither with little intermission. On that eventful morning at 8 we started from Camp near Muddy Branch. How we got ahead of the other Regiments of our Brigade, and crossed on the pontoon bridge over the Potomac at Harper's Ferry, two hours before the rest, you have been informed before. Tuesday, Thursday and Friday I bivouacked, often suffering from cold after the fatigue of marching all day. Near Charlestown, which we reached Wednesday afternoon, I slept in the barn of the rebel Gen. Hunter, and enclosed a relic from his house in one of my letters. At this bivouac the men of the Brigade killed several hogs and sheep. The inhabitants complained, and the officers paid $60 as their share of damages. * * On the march to Perryville few families showed the Union flag. We heard that Banks had entered Winchester and we were ordered back, our services being no longer necessary. Our return march was only diversified by a second march through Charlestown. People looked on in sullen silence, one woman cheering for Jeff. Davis. Owing to fatigue I did not visit the place of John Brown's execution, but we passed the jail and court-house, scenes of his trial and confinement. Saturday noon we reached Bolivar, about one mile from Harper's Ferry, and quartered in the deserted houses. The Ferry is situated in the angle formed by the confluence of the Potomac and the Shenandoah, so famed for beauty. Lofty hills form the banks of either river. Along the Maryland side runs the Chesapeake & Ohio canal, between the Potomac and the Baltimore & Ohio Railroad. On the Virginia side lies the Ferry on the hillside; and on an adjoining hill, Bolivar. These hills were occupied by both rebels and Unionists in attack or defence; while the inhabitants fled to save themselves and their property. A few hundred only remain, while cannon balls and shells scattered here and there, and houses pierced by random shot, attest the former presence of hostile armies. In the Ferry all the government buildings have been reduced to ruins, and their shattered walls looked miserably sad. The engine house, where for days John Brown defied Virginia, is now the prison for rebels.

All the next week it rained, and the streets, cut up by the constant passing of heavy teams, were reduced to a condition rivalling those of Muddy Branch. Friday night orders came to be ready to start at daylight of Saturday. Reveille beat at 4 A. M., and at 5.30 we were in marching order, but after waiting till 10 we were informed that transportation had not arrived, and disgusted we turned back in-doors and rekindled our fires. Saturday and Sunday passed wearily, but in the evening of the latter day we were ordered to be in readiness to start at 7.30 A. M., Monday, and at that hour we left Bolivar for the Ferry. After two hours of tedious waiting we crossed the river on single planks placed end to end along the railroad bridge just completed. The sleepers were wide asunder, the river was swift, the elevation great; but single file, we all crossed in safety. Arrived at Sandy Hook, on the the Maryland side, we waited in the cold till 10 P. M. before the train arrived, and when it came we beheld the freight cars as friends in which we had travelled before. The officers, however, rejoiced in a passenger car, and after a tedious night's travel we arrived in Washington Tuesday noon. We lodged at the Soldiers' Rest, and Wednesday noon we marched to a camp ground in the environs. * * In the afternoon of Thursday we struck tents, packed wagons, and left camp in half an hour after the reception of marching orders. We marched down Pennsylvania avenue about 5.30, amid clouds of dust, to the foot of 6th street, where we took the steamer North America. * * To-day I examined my knapsack and found that some one had appropriated my blouse and pants. They were worn out, but I had intended to send them home as my first uniform. Moreover our seven days' rations were stolen while the cook slept. But such is war, and I feel lucky because I do not lose as much as others. Good night.

The following appeared in the Lynn Transcript of January 19, 1883.

A UNIQUE MUSICAL FESTIVAL.

EDITOR TRANSCRIPT:—

Just now there seems to be a revival of interest in matters relating to the cause of the Great American Rebellion. Dr. James Freeman Clarke began a course of lectures on the Story of Slavery, in Boston on Wednesday evening; and the discourse of Frederick Douglass in Odd Fellows' Hall last week, which I heard with great pleasure, reminded me of an incident in my own experience during the war, which I would like to briefly narrate. It will be remembered that after the first great disaster of Bull Run there was a long period of inaction on the part of the Army of the Potomac, of which the country became very tired and disgusted. President Lincoln ordered the army to move Feb. 22, 1862. Sumner's Corps, in which I was, moved March 12 from its camp at Muddy Branch, up the canal to Harper's Ferry; thence out to join Banks' Division at Winchester. When we got near Charlestown, about 10 miles beyond Harper's Ferry, we bivouacked, and the next morning the whole Division marched through Charlestown and right by the foot of the hill where John Brown was hung. Douglass said the other night, "John Brown was remembered in song." Certainly he was, on the occasion to which I refer. The post of honor that day belonged to the 3d Brigade, on the right of which was the 19th Mass., Col. Hinks. The band struck up the familiar strain—

"John Brown's body lies mouldering in the ground,
His soul goes marching on."

The whole army took up the song, and all day through the streets of the little town tramped 15,000 men singing this memorable refrain. Charlestown was thoroughly "secesh," and though colored folks were out in force, no white people could be seen, except peeping through their closed blinds. As often happens in the army, we were ordered back the next day; and on the countermarch the Charlestowners were treated to a "repeat." We dispensed with the formality of an encore.

J. L. R.

MARCH 31.

'Still on steamer, our destination unknown. * * Friday morning we steamed down the river past Alexandria. The day was delightful, and this part of our passage the pleasantest experience of the 19th since its enlistment. We passed Mt. Vernon, Aquia Creek, Cockpit Point and Fort Washington. A storm of wind arising during the night, we put back several miles to Point Lookout.

HAMPTON, APRIL 1.

We are settled here for a few days. Maryland, our home for eight months past, is left forever as the camping ground of the 19th. We landed at Point Lookout about noon of Saturday, in a snowstorm. We took possession of the deserted hotel, for the season does not begin till June. To the non-commissioned staff was allotted a cottage of two rooms. Barrows [the hospital steward, a son of Prof. Barrows of Andover] and myself, found a dinner at a farm house, and Chesapeake oysters rapidly disappeared from the smoking dishes. The good lady refused compensation, and after a hearty meal we returned to quarters. Sunday morning, the storm having abated, we re-embarked and proceeded down the river. The shores of the Potomac are neither so high, nor cultivated, nor picturesque as those of the Hudson, but the river itself is broader and nobler. Monday morning before breakfast we reached the Fortress, which Ed. Hall has probably described. The Rip Raps and Sewall's Point were in plain sight, the bay was full of shipping of all sizes, shapes and kinds. The Monitor lay at anchor a few rods from our stern. She looks exactly as represented in the papers. At noon we disembarked and marched over a most tedious road, rendered well nigh impassable from the previous rain. The day was very hot, and many fell behind on our short march of five miles to Hampton. We are now quartered a mile beyond the village. You know the rebels burned it before they left, and its appearance is even more desolate than that of Harper's Ferry. Houses and churches are in•ruins, and soldiers only fill the streets and enliven the picture. There are now around here nearly 100,000 men, and eight regiments from Massachusetts (the 2d, 7th, 10th, 17th, 18th, 19th, 20th and 22d.) How long we remain is of course uncertain. Whether we march inland or are transported south, is equally so. How soon I shall be able to write again, or in fact what I have written amid such confusion and interruption, I cannot tell. Pardon haste, pencil and dirt.

Your aff. Brother, ED.

THE PENINSULAR CAMPAIGN.

"He that ruleth his spirit is better than he that taketh a city."—PROVERBS XVI. 32.

The following letter records the death of the "first martyr to liberty" in the 19th Mass.

CAMP NEAR YORKTOWN,

APRIL 8, 1862.

DEAR SISTER:

You have probably received my letter to Charlie long since, hough I cannot remember the day of my mailing it from Hampton. One hundred and twenty-six regiments besides numberless pieces of artillery have been brought together in the vicinity of Fortress Monroe. We at length received orders Thursday to start on the morrow with three days' rations. At 7 next A. M., we gaily started in the rear of two Divisions. For hours before we started, Cavalry, Infantry, and baggage trains had passed along the road in an unbroken stream, impressing one with the vastness of preparations, as only an eye-witness can be impressed. Our march was over the sandy road toward Big Bethel, and after a day's travel, with frequent halts, we bivouacked for the night a mile beyond the town. It had been strongly fortified by the rebels, whose pickets evacuated it as the head of our column entered, some nine hours before. To eyes no more practiced than ours it seemed almost impregnable. Woods and marshes surrounded it, and every approach in front and flank was protected by breastworks and rifle-pits; but Secesh saw fit to leave, and we quietly took possession. Next morning at 5 we started again, and with occasional "double-quicks" had soon made five miles; when, after passing some fortifications whose strength and size excited the wonder of us all, we halted. These earth-works, now becoming very common, are so constructed that one plays into the other, so that, the first being stormed, the second attacks it as our men pour in. This second is raked by a third, and each one successively taken, the garrison retire to support the defence of the next. The country being very woody and swampy, with many small hills, offers every advantage to the defending party.

Here we halted during a rain-storm of several hours. Gen'ls. McClellan and Heintzelman passed us on horseback, as they had done the day before. Little Mac is a great favorite, and as he rode along the lines, the tumultuous cheering growing gradually and constantly louder as he approached, culminating in a deafening roar as he passed, and gradually dying away in the distance, showed us at once the extent of the line and the enthusiasm of the soldiery under such a leader. McClellan is very handsome and every inch a soldier. I never saw such an eye.

The storm had turned the road, which before had been very good, to a continuous slough. Our progress therefore was very slow and uncomfortable; but about 4½ P. M. of Saturday we reached our present bivouac. Sunday being pleasant, Barrows and I went to a farm-house in the woods to breakfast. The women as we approached stared with fright from the windows, and despatched a servant in hot haste to call in the men. But we soon won our way into their regards, and breakfasted on bread and milk, for which we were expected to pay 75 cents; but the hypocrites, who had been so loud in the profession of their Union sentiments, let us off with a tax of 50 cents. At noon we bathed in a neighboring brook. Yesterday we started with the 20th and our Sharpshooters on a reconnoissance. Arrived in a cleared space surrounded by woods we heard the command, "Battalion, Halt — Prepare to load — Load." For the first time we loaded against an enemy yet unseen, and the silence in which the order was obeyed showed the feelings of the men. One company deployed as skirmishers in our front, while we advanced through the woods a minute or two, and finally halted behind a Virginia fence. Here we halted four hours, while engineers and scouts observed and reported. Some of our men advanced a little in front in a series of large fortifications, and played away. The rebels answered, and wasted so much ammunition on the woods; I went down to see the fun, and saw the batteries and the flag of the rebels. The estimated position and strength of the rebels having been made, we were ordered to advance and draw the enemy's fire, to prove the correctness of the estimate ; and on we went, sometimes trying this, sometimes that point, ourselves sheltered by the woods, but enabled to see and shoot the rebels as they appeared The regiment behaved beautifully; but when the first shell burst over our heads as we lay concealed in a gully, a captain started to run for. better shelter, and disturbed the men. However, his indiscretion was at once corrected. Three men were wounded, one of whom died as soon as we reached quarters. It had rained since 11 A. M., and as we picked our way home at 7 P. M., the water fell in torrents. The mud was ankle-deep, and the men had no possible shelter, for we have tents only for field and staff. Thanks to Barrows, I was permitted to sleep on the stretcher which bore a wounded man from the field, and at the foot of the bed whereon he lay a corpse. Off went boots, stockings and pants. I cuddled under a pile of bed-ticks and slept ; but toward morning, when rest had relieved my fatigue, I woke to think on my strange position. But such is the fortune of war, and except in Co. D, to which the deceased belonged, all is joyous as ever. Oh, that men would think of their state and their destiny. But this can be only when they are in full possession of their powers, the very season when they feel least their need. When we come to fight, or to suffer, or to die, the mind has other work, and rarely indeed can it overcome the distractions which surround it. *Our* first martyr to liberty has fallen. To-morrow, or at any rate before this week ends, we attack this fortification, and the result of the struggle none can foresee. This only is sure. If we meet opposition the fight will be very bloody. For myself I fear not, but for the souls who must perish there—what can I do ? God only can save.

All night long it has rained, nor has the storm yet passed over. Our clothes are wet after yesterday's and last night's experiences. .My boot left behind in Washington has not arrived, perhaps will not; and though my hardships are slight in comparison with those of the men, I have suffered more since yesterday morning than since I enlisted (except perhaps at Ball's Bluff). My love to all. As I write this under a rubber blanket supported on stakes, and on the top of a barrel, you must excuse poor writing and mistakes and all imperfections.

EDGAR.

CAMP WINFIELD-SCOTT,
APR. 26, 1862.

DEAR BRO.:

As we go on picket tomorrow, I must write my weekly letter today. * * Yesterday, in obedience to orders, I guided a working party of fifty to the batteries, and opened a road through the woods, some ¼ mile in length. This is (on my part) the " first important operation of the war." Today, though the rain falls in torrents, I am ordered to guide another party to the same place, but they have not yet reported and I hope to escape the job. The particulars of Capt. Bartlett's accident are as follows : He went into an open field to view the enemies' batteries, and while kneeling on the ground with the glass in his hands, a ball struck him above the knee, passing downward and so shattering the joint as to render amputation necessary. We all feel sorry, but our life is one of such constant danger that an accident creates far less stir here than the news of it at home. This morning at 5, we were turned out, from fire occasioned by the 1st Mass· taking a rebel rifle pit several miles below us. In a few hours the men returned wet through, shortly after I had completed my toilet, for I slept so well that not even the heavy firing awoke me. Vague rumors of an approaching paymaster, but we are very sceptical. I have several times purchased 50 cents worth of eatables with a dollar bill yet remaining in my possession, because no one could change it.

After dinner—the rain still continues. Owing to its depressing influence, and my dinner of crackers fried in maggoty bacon and served up in molasses, my stomach exhibits unmistakable symptoms of dissatisfaction.

Our army corps (the centre) will probably engage the enemy only to divert them from the right, where lies Yorktown upon which the main assault will be made, and where Heintzelman's corps is massed together. There is a rumor at Head-quarters of our Regiment being sent to Burnside, where it was first going, if McClellan had permitted. I am delighted to hear of the reception of our Quartermaster's order for my trunk, as I have lost so much lately it seemed but natural the trunk should follow. All quiet on the lower Potomac.

EDGAR.

THE 19TH MASS. TAKES POSSESSION OF REBEL WORKS AT YORKTOWN.

YORKTOWN, MAY 6, 1862.

DEAR LEILA:

Yorktown has been evacuated, and I write this on board the Steamer Vanderbilt, now lying off Yorktown, about to start with the 19th and 20th for West Point to intercept the Rebels' retreat. Our future seven days promise to be so full of work that I take this opportunity of writing, uncertain when I can find another. Last Saturday our Brigade was on picket at our ordinary picket post in the woods, about 1¼ miles from the enemy's batteries. My duties as guide requiring me to be present at camp rather than in the woods, I had not of late accompanied the Reg't, but as shot and shell had been freely changed between us and our foes all day long, I determined to spend the night in the woods, expecting fun, and slept without waking but twice, partially owing to the fatigue consequent on having visited all the batteries along our line during the afternoon. Capt. Rice and I met in an open field within rifle shot of the forts which frowned upon us, threatening every moment to shoot, but fearing the Andrew Sharpshooters, who filled the rifle pit which partially protected us. The explosion of gunpowder, too, had become so common that, though it occurred every fifteen minutes during the night, I knew it not till next A. M. Before I turned out, news came that three contrabands came into our lines (which by the way are opposite Winn's Mills) and reported that Secesh had "skedaddled," and that other niggers were seeking our protection in the woods. Lieut. Hume, Co. K., being sent with one nigger to find these last, made instead a double-quick to the rebel works, and mounting the parapet, swung his hat and cheered lustily. At once the Col. ordered our pickets forward, and the 19th—first of all the Division, and I know not of how many other Divisions along the line—planted its State and U. S. flags on the ramparts. A body of cavalry soon followed us to post its pickets; the 19th was ahead, and it yielded. Soon we heard cheering and knew the whole Regiment had possessed themselves of the works. Soon as possible (for the Col. had once refused me permission) I entered the works. They were of the strongest character, but proofs for the men, a kind of citadel overlooking and protecting by rifles the heavier works and guns below. In front was a long stretch of marshy land, which with the ditch could be completely overflowed from the mill-pond above. Within was a succession of rifle-pits of every size and angle with each other, and each raking the one in front. Under the most favorable circumstances it could not have been captured without immense loss, as each fort protected the other, and the ones at York-town and Warwick all the rest. It would first have been necessary to flank them by gunboats, and this even, to any unpractised eye, was almost impossible.

We scouted through the woods till our foremost descried the rebel cavalry, the rear guard of the retreating foe. On one tent was written, " We can whip twice our number of Yankees; " and on the next, in characters clearer and more legible from their less age, " He that fights and runs away, will live to fight another day. May 3." (The night of the evacuation.) About a mile from the forts toward Yorktown stood the house of the rebel Gen'l. Hill. Everything had been sent away except the piano; the mansion was the most beautiful I have seen in Virginia. Below was the dairy through which flowed a stream of the coolest and finest water.

A little further on in the woods lay the deserted camp of a Brigade. Tents were left pitched; camp-fires left burning; food, arms and equipments strewed around in the confusion of their departure. I gathered a few relics which I will send to Boston as soon as possible. At noon came orders to hold ourselves in readiness to march. We fell in at once, but no farther orders arriving, bivouacked for the night at our old camp. Monday at 1 A. M. it began to rain, and 9 A. M. found us on the march to Yorktown, in mud and water. At noon we arrived before the city and pitched our shelter tents. Before us stretched the long fortifications of Yorktown. Immediately in front was the breast-work which Washington built to protect his troops; and fifty rods further on, the spot where he received Cornwallis' sword 81 years ago.

The rain had fallen almost without intermission since Monday

A. M. Every road leading to Yorktown was crowded with Cavalry, Artillery and baggage wagons. The firing of the gunboats (as they poured shot and shell into the flank of the retreating foe) and sounds of distant musketry made the whole scenery and suggestion mateal in the extreme. At 6 P. M., in the midst of a smart shower, we struck tents and marched again. The roads grew inconceivably heavy to one who has never witnessed them after rain and travel have done their work. Wagons broke down, horses stuck, and such was the delay that in eight hours we had made but two miles. Once I lost my rubber boot. An orderly following rescued it after a severe struggle, and I proceeded barefoot in the rain to the nearest fire, and having washed the member restored the boot. So weary were we that men lay down in the mud to sleep at every halt, and when we at last turned off the road at 2 this A. M., I spread my blankets on which the rain had poured all day, and slept without interruption till daylight. I woke neither stiff nor cold. To-day we lay on the beach till 3 P. M., when we left for West Point. Men with no military knowledge can see how careless or ignorant must be the General who orders 5000 men or more into a muddy road at 6 of a stormy night, to march a distance of two miles to a point where he cannot possibly use them till morning, and, as the result proved, till 3 next P. M. But Generals don't go afoot nor carry knapsacks, nor lack shelter, or wood for fire, or servants to build it. How can they feel? But our commissioned officers (from Col. down) must now suffer with the privates deprivation of food, sleep and fire; *but they don't stand it.* I thought I had little endurance, but these gentry have been almost every one sick from exposure, while I not at all, my near approach to sickness being caused by miasma.

But to describe Yorktown, which I visited this morning. A church and one-half dozen houses are all the original town. Secesh has erected numerous and expensive buildings for army purposes. His works of defence and offence, both here and at Gloucester Point just opposite, are strong and magnificent. Indeed no pains or expense is spared in his work. Immense military stores have been abandoned, and the large siege guns spiked. He has strewn torpedoes everywhere. The machine being buried all except the head, which is too small to be readily perceived, explodes under the incautious soldier's foot and hurls him into eternity. Two score perhaps have been killed in this fiendish manner since Sunday. McClellan, as reported in the New York Herald of yesterday, compelled evacuation by the evident superiority of his works; I believe rather by the superiority of his strategy. Magruder is reported to have fled for fear of losing his connections

with Richmond; which you will find quite probable. * * Steamboat
jars, confusion reigns, and I feel sleepy. Our recent great successes
have inspired me with strength and feelings unknown before. With
God is all the glory, who has seemed not to suffer us to conquer, so
much as to have confounded their counsels.

EDGAR.

DESCRIPTION OF A BATTLE.

> " By regiment! Forward into line!"
> Then sabres and guns and bayonets shine.
> Oh ye who feel your fate at last,
> Repeat the old prayers, as your hearts beat fast!
> Rub-a-dub-dub! Rub-a-dub-dub!

ELTHAM, MAY 11, 1862.

DEAR BROTHER:

My last letter was written on board the steamer which conveyed
us to a place a few miles below West Point. We arrived about 6
P. M., Tuesday, and anchored for the night. Next day about noon
we debarked. A sharp skirmish had begun in the woods and fields
about a mile from the landing, and we were immediately detached
from the Brigade as a reserve. Here on the open field bordering the
river, we passed an afternoon, where I learned more of a battle in its
entireness than I ever shall again. Imagine a meadow almost level,
twenty times as large as our common, bordered on three sides by
woods; on the fourth by the York river. Regiments constantly pour
in from the landing, and take their places in close order by divisions
i. e., five lines parallel to each other and six paces apart, 1000 men
being thus contracted into the smallest possible space known to military science ; 15 or more regiments, besides several batteries of
artillery, are posted thus, ready at a moment's notice to start for the
battle field. We hear the continuous rattle of musketry and the cheers
of the combatants, as alternately they gain temporary advantage and
press their adversaries back. In the centre of the meadow are the
Head-quarters of Gen. Slocum in temporary command of all our forces.
Mounted on his horse he receives the messages which officers of the
Signal Corps telegraph from the battle ground through the chain of
sentries who, posted a few rods from each other, pass the messages
along; he despatches his aides with orders to the commanders of gunboats, batteries and infantry forces. Two batteries, each supported
by a regiment of infantry, are drawn up in line and playing on our
unseen foe, while the gunboats on the river throw shell far over our
heads, where the reserve of the enemy is supposed to be posted. Add
to this that parties of men are constantly bearing in the dead and
wounded on stretchers to the hospital in our rear, and the picture is

complete. But one must experience the reality to appreciate the impatience with which we waited the command to advance, and the disappointment which I felt at learning, on awaking from a doze in the hot sun, that Secesh had withdrawn. They fear our gunboats, and though shot and shell had fallen thick around our fleet (one even passing through the smokestack of the Vanderbilt, where Manning who was sick had remained) yet a few hundred pound shell from these low black craft made John Reb withdraw his batteries on the double quick.

I have had no fresh meat for two weeks; nothing but hard bread and coffee for three days. Strict orders compelled us to rise at 3 A. M. This morning Manning came up with his haversack full of veal. No questions were asked, but the veal was very good. The enemy can be perceived throwing up earth works ahead, but I fear that, after having been so near a battle again and again, we shall finally return without having seen even the rebels' backs. My health is excellent, and I am daily lost in wondering gratitude for such merciful preservation. Most of the officers are rarely well of late, while I am more rarely unwell. Perhaps these long weary years of abstinent self-denial are beginning to bear fruit. The paymaster has been here and paid us for January and February. Enclosed is a Secesh letter which I picked up in a rebel encampment last Sunday. Press it out and give it to Stanley for me. I hope sister and James are well, and while you are in Sabbath school, I bid you good bye.

EDGAR.

Capt. Newman informs us that "Chaplain E. D. Winslow was left at Eltham, by orders of the Colonel, in charge of the sick, and other matters pertaining to the Regiment." This circumstance led to an interesting event which is recorded on a subsequent page.

Soon after the letter of May 11th was written Newcomb became unwell, and did not fully recover until after the battle of Fair Oaks, May 31 and June 1, 1862. Capt. Stephen J. Newman (then Principal Musician) writes as follows: "At camp at Laurel Hill, Va., May 20th, he was delirious from fever. I made him take shelter with me from the storm, but he never gave up a moment from duty. I brought the Surgeon to him, and insisted that he should be excused from duty. But no; Edgar would not; and next morning, wet to the skin and without breakfast, he was at his duty."

A HOSPITAL VISIT.

MAY. 24, 1862.

DEAR SISTER:

At length after two days of hard but fatiguing marching with only 24 hours' interval, we are arrived at a nameless camp within 13 miles of Richmond. The men are sick of soldiering, the intermitted order for 3 A. M. rising having been again enforced; rations being exceedingly poor, and 121 of our Regiment absent, 109 from sickness. Even I, who till within a week never had a thought of homesickness, want to go home and get something to eat. And notice, once at home I'll never go again for a soldier. No fresh hardships, nor the continuance of hardships, have changed me; but the prize of health is gained. My position is not as agreeable as it was, or might now be, and I only want to enter Richmond, and then "good evening, Mr. Soldier," as they say here. Months I fear must elapse before we are mustered out of service. We have marched hard and far to catch a sight of the backs even of the rebels, but so far in vain.

Manning went into the hospital this morning. Last night a piece of Bologna gave his weak stomach a most violent cholic. You are probably expecting it to be a cool quiet place in pleasant weather, warm and dry in wet, and generally inviting. When I went to see him, I found in a huge canvas tent two rows of sick men, feet to feet, dying on the damp ground, which was drained by a trench dug between the rows of patients. Such are the accommodations of a 'Regimental field hospital. If the patient convalesces and becomes well, good; if not, he is sent to Monroe. Manning will probably be out in a few days, but one so tenderly reared, so young and sympathetic and impulsive, is apt to sink at once to the most dismal homesickness.

Col Hinks has given his permission to hold a prayer-meeting to-morrow, the weather permitting; so we shall have something to remind us of the good old times we once knew, and the good times we hope again to know.

You probably would like to know about our marches. We left Cedar Hill about 8 A. M., three days ago, and marched till the middle of the afternoon, being some eight hours on the road under an intensely hot sun; stopping only when the artillery and baggage ahead became blocked, resting nowhere long enough for dinner. Twelve miles was our march, and one-third of the Regiment fell out. Next day came an order that any man falling out of the march should receive no whiskey for the next 24 hours. Yesterday the sun didn't shine, but the atmosphere was most oppressive. However, not one to my knowledge fell out. Indeed, the half gill of whiskey served out every morning and night seems to be all that relieves the monotony of the life of the Regiment.

Yesterday we passed several splendid farms. On the gates leading to the magnificent mansions were white flags, and the strict orders against leaving the ranks prevented all depredation or purchase; and here let me return to our commissary department, for I know the satisfaction of gratified appetite. During the cold season of more than six months we never knew a single issue of bacon; but now from the time we left Monroe, bacon, clear fat, has been served out regularly, and generally to the exclusion of salt beef. The men cannot eat it at this time. Yet it is generally the only meat served out. So fare Uncle Sam's.

We are now encamped by the roadside, a swamp all around. We dig wells, and before they reach five feet in depth they are filled. The rain of today has saturated the ground like a sponge. As I overheard one say just now, "A man here doesn't know where to stop; he goes to his tent, but it looks so desolate he doesn't dare go into it." If the men did not expect soon to go home, their sufferings would be almost intolerable. It seems to take a long time for letters to reach me now. It seems to me that if you could be so regular in writing when I was comparatively comfortable, you might continue the practice now that we are so thoroughly miserable.

EDGAR.

Newcomb's illness, previously mentioned, doubtless increased his despondency at this time. He devoted no little attention to the sick and wounded, and the hospital visit above mentioned was only one out of many.

A MILITARY FUNERAL.

"There is no discharge in that war." Ecclesiastes VIII. 8.
"Present—arms. Shoulder—arms. Reverse—arms. Column forward. March."
Infantry Tactics (funeral honors.)
"Marching to the plaintive cry of fifes—it is almost a woman's wail—and the moan of muffled drums." Taylor.

Nathaniel Prentiss of Cambridge enlisted in the 19th Mass. Vols. in August, 1861. He was mustered in at Lynnfield as Sergeant in Co. F. At that time he was 34 years of age, stalwart and apparently in excellent health. At Camp Benton, early in November, 1861, he was transferred to the Commissary Department, and soon after was appointed Quartermaster Sergeant. The severe experiences on the Peninsula were very trying to the most robust, and any latent weakness of constitution was sure to be revealed. Prentiss died suddenly on May 25, 1862, at Lewis Farm, near Cold Harbor, Va. Capt. Newman gives the following particulars: "He was found dead in his tent by Edgar. I think he must have died from heart disease; for our (22) Army Corps only reached that camp near Cold Harbor at 7.30 P. M. of the previous day. The Quartermaster Sergeant was on the sick report for about a week, but managed to do his duty."

About six months before this sad event, Newcomb wrote an account of the burial of a comrade, deprived of even a religious service, for the Chaplain was away. "It sickens me," he continues, "to live in such an atmosphere. Man lives and dies like a brute." On the present occasion the Chaplain was also absent in obedience to orders. Newcomb very properly decided to act as Chaplain *pro tempore*, in order that the remains of Prentiss might have Christian burial. Newcomb and Prentiss were originally members of the same company, and since promotion they had passed many pleasant hours together as Non-Commissioned Staff Officers.

It was somewhat difficult to find a suitable place for the grave. Near the Chichahoming the ground was too wet, and a location was selected at some distance from the stream. A detail was ordered to prepare the grave, and considerable labor was expended in digging through the coarse gravel and stone.

The funeral took place on May 27th, and Capt. Stephen J. Newman has kindly furnished interesting details which are given below: "Edgar read from the scripture, St. John, 'I am the resurrection', &c.—the Lord's Prayer (and let me say here that I never heard before a more fervent recital of the Lord's Prayer):—Co. F. was detailed as the funeral party, with all the other men of the Regiment that wished to attend:—Sixteen men and a Sergeant, as firing party:—Location of the grave, about half a mile from camp, and nearer to Cold Harbor, and about 100 yards from the road; to the right and rear of the old mill at Cold Harbor:—Funeral about 10.30 A. M:—Dead March in Saul, by all the field (20) music:—Coffin lowered in grave by the usual military honors [see Newcomb's letter of Nov. 23, 1861]:—weather, fair:—Dress parade in the eve. Edgar was Sergeant Major, and never absent from his post at any time to my knowledge."

In a subsequent letter Capt. Newman states that "Co. F funeral party was in charge of the 1st Sergeant; and the funeral escort was in command of the Senior Sergeant of Co. F. The obsequies was under the immediate orders and charge of the Officer of the Day." Capt. Newman also refers to Newcomb's excellent remarks "over the remains of our Comrade Prentiss," and adds: "Edgar may have acted as Chaplain after I left the Regiment; I was discharged at Warrentown, Va., Nov. 10, 1862, and bade Edgar adieu at 2 P. M. that day. Edgar gave me one-half the money he had to pay my expenses, $5, to Washington."

In his letters Newcomb did not mention his prominent part at the funeral. Diligent inquiry has failed to bring to light any other instance in which Edgar considered it his duty to perform the *public* functions of Chaplain. His voluntary service in the absence of the proper officer was not without precedent at an early period in the war, as will be seen below.

The 13th Mass. Vols. went to the front somewhat in advance of the 19th, and Companies A and B were posted on Antietam Creek, not far from the locality where the famous battle was afterwards fought. On Sunday, Aug. 18, 1861, a correspondent of the Boston *Journal* wrote as follows: "In the absence of our regular Chaplain, Brevet Major Fox officiated. The services consisted of reading a chapter from the New Testament; selections from the Psalms; reading a portion of the Episcopal church service; repeating the Lord's Prayer. Simple as this service may seem, it was the most impressive to me that I have witnessed since we have been organized. At the conclusion of our religious ceremonies Major Fox commenced the reading of the Articles of War, but before he had time to go through them, Col. Leonard arrived." A complete history of the terrible struggle would include many incidents similar to those above narrated. In one case a woman read the burial service over the remains of a brave young officer, as it was impossible to secure the presence of a Chaplain or any other man who was willing to undertake the duty. The solemn yet beautiful scene has been depicted in verse.

Cold Harbor, or Cold Arbor, has been a summer resort for the people of Richmond for nearly a hundred years. A portion of the forces under McClellan and Grant struggled against superior numbers of the enemy near this place, in 1862 and 1864. In June, 1866, the remains of Union soldiers buried in surrounding fields were re-interred in the National cemetery at Cold Harbor.

In regard to Newcomb's qualifications for the performance of sacred duties Col. Chadwick remarks that he would have made an excellent Chaplain.

A few days after the funeral of Prentiss, thousands of men were killed and wounded at Seven Pines and Fair Oaks. "The 19th was in reserve at Fair Oaks, but under fire," as Capt. Wm. A. Hill informs us. Further particulars concerning the desperate fight on Saturday and Sunday, May 31 and June 1, are given in Newcomb's letter dated June 5, 1862. It will be observed that the regiment was within a few miles of the Confederate capital.

CAMP BEFORE RICHMOND,

JUNE 5, 1862.

DEAR LEILA :

Here we are more than a mile on the northern side of the Chickahominy, which the Reg't crossed Saturday 5½ miles from Richmond, and on the eve of a most fearful fight. In my last I told you how the 19th was on picket, and I staid at camp; how I heard firing, but determined to stay and have a good night's sleep. All the afternoon and night, Infantry, Artillery, ammunition and ambulance wagons hurried past as if mad. Sunday morning came orders for all serviceable men to join the Reg't. About 6 A. M. I crossed the creek; the current is swift, the banks for ¼ mile on either side are an impassable and an impenetrable swamp. No better barrier for defence could be selected, but we crossed it Saturday without opposition, and then Secesh tried to drive us back. That afternoon they were temporarily successful. Sedgwick's Division arrived just in time, and the 7th Michigan drove them back, or rather kept them from driving us farther. Sunday the creek began to rise, swollen either by the rain four hours before, or by the breaking down of dams the rebels had constructed for the purpose of flooding us; and by night the bridge constructed the previous day with so much labor was all swept away. Even the field ¼ mile from the creek, where our Reg't lay when I joined them, was covered with 30 inches of water. Sunday morning the firing recommenced. About 8, we were ordered forward a mile or so, drawn up in a beautiful wood, arms were stacked, and the men lay down to rest.

About noon orders came from the Brigadier to move forward. For a space of two miles we travelled at a rapid rate over ploughed land and gravelled roads. Here I saw the first stones I had seen since Fortress Monroe. Mud, brooks and swamps, and when we were at last halted, breathless and perspiring profusely under the hot mid-day sun, 'twas only to receive orders from the Major-General to return to our old quarters, the woods. So we left the wounded, and the hospitals and the firing, and at a pace equally rapid returned. The rebels were slowly driven back Sunday and at 6 P.M. we were ordered again to the front. Such alas, is the fate of the 19th. If in front, the enemy run (as at Yorktown); if behind, we are not needed. We bivouacked a few hundred yards from our halting place of a few hours before, and about one hundred from the battle-field of the two days past, the woods on our front and right. These were full of dead. About 9, quick firing was heard in the woods, and we turned out at once. But it proved to be one party of our pickets firing on another. Three men were killed as we learned next day. No further alarm during the night. Next day we were ordered to furnish a detail to bury the dead. They worked till noon, when we were ordered to the front, immediately in rear of the pickets where we now are. Many officers and men visited the woods and hospitals from curiosity. They report the scenes as sickening. The dead, lying exposed to the air, often in piles of fifteen or more, for two days, had become swollen and offensive. All attitudes, and contortions and wounds were present. In one place part of a company were shot down, each by a wound immediately mortal. There they lay in two ranks, and file-closers, their heels on the very spot where they stood and fought. Most of these dead were rebels. Most of ours and the wounded had been already brought in, but occasionally one of the wounded was carried past to the crowded hospital.

We occupy now the camp from which the rebels were driven Sunday. It is low, and surrounded by the graves of the dead. Frequent shelling and firing on our pickets, almost within sight in the woods ahead, have disturbed our rest by day and night. An almost uninterrupted and very severe rain has flooded the ground and wet us through, for we marched without knapsacks or tents. An overcoat and woollen blanket are all the protection we have against water. My feet have been wet ever since Sunday noon. Our rations are a scant allowance of hard bread, coffee twice a day (though last night we had none at all), occasionally fresh or salt beef. Nothing else, and this for a victorious army beside the railroad which we hold and run from West Point here. I don't blame Uncle Sam or little Mac, but some commissary of the Brigade, Division or Corps, who has little energy and less humanity. * * In answer to your question the 19th was the first of our Division, and second of the whole army to plant the Stars and Stripes on the rebel works; a regiment of Smith's Division on our left being first of all the line.

JUNE 6.

Knowing your anxiety, I shall if possible forward this today. I am perfectly well, after this the third day's exposure to a constant rain. The news of the last fight begins to reach us, and we find it more terrible than we had supposed. As soon as possible after the 19th have had their turn, I will write, but we can make no advance till return of fine weather. * *

JUNE 7.

Yesterday I was ordered to return to our old camp for some papers. I went down on the train which conveyed the wounded soldiers home. How I wished I was wounded slightly. In the cattle car with myself were 30 wounded, and as their wounds had begun to maturate and were constantly exposed—partly from pride, partly to relieve and cool their feverishness—the stench was intolerable, and here for the first time did I appreciate the meaning of "the sickening details of war." Men were shot in the breast, arms, legs, head. Many were the amputations. One fellow had a ball through his breast, and an arm shot off.

But I managed to survive and reach a despatch station, from which I footed it to camp, three miles. This morning at 5½ A. M., I was on my way to camp. I returned on foot, travelling at least 7 miles without breakfast and over the vilest of roads. We have to corduroy two-thirds of the roads here. Arrived in camp I found the regiment under marching orders. From the disposition of troops in our rear, a fight was evidently expected. I ate a very hearty breakfast of stewed beans, hard bread and coffee, and then read your letters which await-my arrival. How glad I am to hear from home constantly. * * All day we have expected an attack or a move, but remain in our old place. Health and spirits are good. As the mail is closing, and my letter has been very long, and there is no more news, I bid you good evening; wishing as I never wished before to spend Saturday night at home, and Sunday in the Christian way.

EDGAR.

FAIR OAKS, JUNE 14, 1862.

DEAR BROTHER:

Two weeks to-day since the battle which has rendered suddenly famous this obscure railroad station. Our camp ground has been changed from the swamp to one of the many burial grounds of this vicinity. The weather has changed from constant rain to intense heat, 6 A. M. being as hot as one of our August mornings at 11. Every morning we rise at 3, remain under arms till 4.30, when we are allowed to turn in. But by that time cooks, wood-choppers and teamsters are noisily at work; and he is fortunate who can sleep, and most to be envied who can both sleep and find any coffee left on awaking. This early rising is most unpleasant and wearing, but at the same time most essential to prevent surprise from a foe who never sleeps. With the exception of two hours' office work, I now do no duty; while the extreme heat and frequent interruptions to sleep, both accidental (i. e., where pickets fire on an imaginary foe, rousing at once for an hour 10 or 12,000 men), and constant (like the 3 A. M. order) dispose me to as little exertion as possible. Nevertheless, while the sweat pours down, and heat-rash and wood-ticks make indescribable itchings over my body, I can do duty with any one. Indeed mere existence seems such a pleasure that I daily wonder and thank God for it. Our life is hard, even for us accustomed to hard living, and we daily experience scenes which it would sicken you to hear me recount—scenes incidental to the camp-life of a victorious army encamped on an extended battle-ground. But we all look forward to Richmond as the goal of our efforts, and, as many think, the termination of our service. Certainly, vast and important changes will be wrought in our regiment before it leaves Richmond to prosecute the war.

Our food is now abundant. The bacon and ham have ceased. A little providence when beans and rice are served out will secure enough for four or five meals. * * Manning, who is an excellent cook, fries pancakes of flour, salt and water, which relish well with molasses or sugar bought from our Commissary. None of our dishes are very recherche, but any change of diet is at once palatable and refreshing. When I shall return I cannot tell, but shall think myself happy to celebrate New Year's day with you. When we march, our course is full of incidents; when we halt, all is still and uneventful. So I have nothing more to write to-day, and wish you a pleasant Sabbath.

EDGAR.

OUR HERO IS IN GREAT PERIL.

CAMP NEAR FAIR OAKS, JUNE 25, 1862.

DEAR CHARLIE:

Last Saturday at 11 P. M. we were roused and marched to the front, forming line behind the parapet. Here we remained till this morning, suffering frequent alarms at all hours of the day and night. Two nights ago we heard a sharp fire in the woods ahead. All hands were at once under arms and most interested auditors of the contest. The shouts of the rebels drew nearer, and we thought surely the contest had come to us, but the rebels contented themselves with holding the entire wood. Here let me explain the position. First is our line of earthworks, a breastwork outside of which is a ditch, and at proper distances along the line are redoubts pierced for cannon. These earthworks extend along our whole line of a dozen miles or more. Just in front of us is an open field formed by felling trees—at once a defence to us and an annoyance to thĕ advancing enemy. Beyond the woods lies an open country where are the earthworks of the enemy. The woods are the disputed ground. About 7.30 this A. M., after seeing several regiments enter the woods, and hearing heavy firing immediately after, we were ordered forward. We filed along through the densest foliage I ever saw. Soon we came across a rebel shot a week or two ago. The gray uniform clothed a skeleton. The firing was now on our right, now in front, now on our left. It was impossible to see fifty feet ahead, and skirmishers were thrown out in front. We marched forward and halted every few minutes till within sight of the line of battle. Lieut. Warner of Co. H was sent forward to learn the exact position and name of our friends. He ran forward through the hot fire and returned in safety, but five minutes after, while he was the centre of a group of three, Lieut. Thorndike being on the right, and I on the left, touching him with my elbow, a stray shot pierced his breast. With a sharp cry he fell and expired. We carried him to the rear and marched on. Soon the enemy, discovering our position, fired volley after volley, which most of our men returned at once without waiting for orders. Few sought to run, and those stopped at the command of the officers who, they knew, would shoot them if they disobeyed. The rattle of musketry was so incessant that it was with difficulty we could hear orders. Soon the left of the company in whose rear is my position discerned men coming in on our flank. We heard the cries of the exulting rebels, as driving us back their shouts grew louder. Visions of a Richmond prison flitted before me as I retreated to find the regiment which had changed position without my knowledge. On I hasted away from the shouts till I saw our welcome flag again. The Major wanted to know what was going on, and as soon as I told him we were retreating the regiment was ordered forward. We arrived just in time to prevent the breaking of some New Jersey troops. For ten or fifteen minutes we were exposed to a constant rain of bullets. The men lay down, but some who remained standing escaped, while others at their feet were wounded. Standing, sitting or lying, the shot seemed to strike without distinction. * * At length we returned, having driven the rebels completely out of the woods in front, with a loss to us of 43, of whom 5 are killed and 4 mortally wounded. The firing continues at intervals, and probably the rebels will make desperate efforts to re-take the woods; but I trust that the same God who has kept me amid the dangers of to-day will still keep me. Death has lost its terrors to most of us, because we have faced it in so many forms and so often. Falling by a hostile bullet and being abandoned by the advancing line, perhaps to die and rot undiscovered in the woods or swamps, that I fear ; but otherwise I welcome death as infinite gain.

Never did I know before how hard it is to fight. It is not the marching nor the firing that wears men, but the suspense of the slow advance and frequent halt, the increasing rattle of musketry, the devilish yells of our merciless enemy; till finally when at once the storm of bullets whirs over and on each side, and men begin to fall, and orders come thick and fast, the sweat oozes from every pore. It is not fear but uncertainty, that so strains the nerves and makes men live days in every moment. I am tired and want to sleep, but our numerous batteries are shelling the space beyond the woods, and I cannot sleep. By the way, Manning followed the regiment, and from fatigue leaned his head against a tree, when a volley swept over him, one ball piercing the tree. Lieut. Hume, Co. K, received two balls through his coat, neither of them wounding him. Our regiment behaved nobly.

JUNE 26th.

Nothing of importance has transpired since yesterday. The woods are now being felled and rifle pits constructed at favorable points. The rebels attempted to capture one last night, but were repulsed with much loss. Your brother, EDGAR.

In the long letter of July 4, Newcomb gives as good an idea as language can convey, of the dangers and sufferings of the 19th during the Seven Days' Retreat. He records the bravery of his comrades, but does not refer to his own conspicuous heroism at White Oak Swamp and elsewhere.

CAMP AT HARRISON'S LANDING, JULY 4, 1862.

DEAR SISTER:

Writing as I do in haste I find I have begun on the last page which please excuse. Thank God, we are at last encamped on the banks of the James, to which for four successive nights we have retreated, leaving on the battle-fields and in the hands of the rebels more than 100 men. I am perfectly safe and sound, though wearied out with the duties of the last week. Saturday morning, June 28, we were informed that a large force was moving on us in four lines. Gen. Hooker on our left sent word he could hold his position if we maintained ours. Immediately we began preparations for defence, adding to the strength of our fortifications by huge traverses. Saturday evening we had orders to be ready to move at a minute's notice, and all night long we were broken of rest by expectation of hearing from the enemy or receiving marching orders. Sunday morning we left at daybreak, and retreated 1½ miles to one of those long undulating fields surrounded by woods, in which Virginia abounds, and which are so perfectly fitted for defence. Regiment after regiment and batteries of artillery filed in till the spacious field was filled, except the side toward the enemy which was commanded at every point. After an hour or two of anxious waiting, we heard the cheers of Secesh. An hour after men came running in and reported them advancing in swarms. Soon musketry was heard in the woods in front. Their pickets had attacked ours. The firing increased as the enemy advanced, till there was a perfect roar as our first line engaged them. Then our batteries opened, throwing shell far over the heads of our men into the reserves of the enemy with terrific effect. We were the second line, but as the first had kept them at bay so well with the assistance of the artillery, we did not advance, and had only to encounter their shells which exploded constantly before, behind and on both sides of us, and above us. The hospitals were soon filled, the dead being left in the woods. At 3 P. M., as the baggage had gained much distance, the artillery limbered up. The pickets were withdrawn and we started almost double-quick for a high hill and plain at its base. The rebels were after us, and their forces kept in sight of our rear guard. All the sick and wounded were brought with us to this place, Savage's Station. Our troops were again disposed in positions. We had not been here an hour before firing in the woods in front warned us they had come up; and a gun posted so as to greatly annoy us caused an order from Meagher's Brigade to advance and take it at the charge. The green flag of Ireland and the Stars and Stripes waved together over three regiments of Irishmen on the double-quick down the hill. In the plain they stripped off knapsacks and entered the woods. Soon the increasing roar told us they had found the foe, and shortly after their cheering told that they were driving him back. But they reached the open space only to find that Secesh had just hauled off their piece. The firing now became more general, the roar of artillery and clatter of small arms almost deafening. One or two lines formed in the woods and two in the plain below. Only two regiments of our Brigade remained on the hill. Ours was one. So far the second time that day we just escaped a fight. About 9 P. M. the artillery limbered up and left. The lines withdrew, and we started in the rain on an eight mile march. So silently did we go that our own pickets were surprised at coming in to find us gone, and our rear guard marched three hours before catching up. By day-break we had put Cedar Swamp creek between us and our foe. Here we halted till 7 A. M. Monday, and then continued our march, blowing up or burning the bridge in our rear. This day like the preceding was oppressively hot. We marched all the forenoon and halted in an open field. About 4 P. M. we heard artillery, the enemy had arrived in front, and sought to cross the swamp. Back we marched 1½ miles and waited further orders. In an hour we were ordered to return to our original position. About half way we were ordered to fix bayonets. Something is up, thought we, and before long began the rattle of muskets and we were on the double-quick. Artillery swept past us, reckless of life or limb. Soon we reached our old ground, but instead of filing to the left, filed to the right, and having formed line before the battery charged down to support the 15th Mass. The bullets flew thick and fast, and having recovered our breath and the confusion of going so far on the double-quick, we entered another field where we saw none ahead of us. Here we lay down behind a knoll and sheltered ourselves somewhat, but stray shots had killed some, and we passed several ghastly corpses. The lines were formed as usual, we being the third. After the two in front had entered the woods we advanced almost to their edge and lay down. Soon Gen. Grover, who for some unknown reason commanded us, ordered us to enter the woods. "Be sure, boys, and don't fire on your own men," were his last words before we entered. Advancing some 150 yards we had halted and dressed, when a regiment hidden by foliage, but not 15 feet distant, opened a terrific fire upon us. The powder flashed in my face and struck my eyes. We retreated but rallied on the edge of the woods, the right charging bayonets; the left not hearing the order still advanced, but only prepared to fire again. Again we retreated before our unexpected foe, and found out next day our friends had marched to the right, and the enemy had advanced to their position. We retreated and formed line again before the woods, but with diminished numbers, entering with more than 300, and returning with 150. Soon a regiment was discovered forming behind the fence in the woods. "Who are you," shouted the Col. No answer. " Fire!" and we fired. They returned it. The Col. was wounded, and the Major fell, and the regiment broke again, but so perfectly are we drilled that the officers soon rallied them. Back we went to our old position, and night fell on us. Companies felt sad, as they looked around upon the few that remained; 6 in Co. H, 7 in Co. F, &c.; 134 men in the regiment, and all the Field Officers gone, with the Senior Captain too. Capt. Rice was in command of the regiment. Putnam of his company was slightly wounded in the shoulder, and being ordered to the hospital cried " Good bye, boys. Give it to them. I'll soon be with you." * * We lay in our old position till 11 P. M., when we withdrew, formed in line of battle till the artillery had passed, so near were we to the enemy who were expected at once to attack us. But they had suffered too severely; and in silence we pursued our retreat, passing through the woods, steep banks on each side of our gloomy road. The men rarely whispered, and answered no questions. But by day-break of Tuesday we entered the opening, and all hands breathed more freely. Thank God, we were safe. As we started a few hours after for our present position, the enemy opened fire from the woods, and we must form again to resist him. He brought a battery to bear upon our lines, and after several men had been killed we changed our position to the woods where we remained all Tuesday. About 3 A. M. of Wednesday we moved, as our men had driven the enemy several miles back the previous evening, and the space before our lines being left open as a trap, had not been occupied by them. By 7 A. M. it began to rain; and I, wearied out with fighting all day and marching all night, and having had little sleep since Friday, soon fell behind the regiment. History will fail to record how the first born son of a " very respectable family " tramped along behind the regiment. No blankets on his back, for they were lost in the first fight; no clothes in his knapsack, - for it failed to go on the teams; few hard bread in his handkerchief, for his haversack had " gone up " two days before; no scabbard to his sword, for that had gone up, too; how, wearied out, he lay down in the rain and slept amid the tramping of foot and the rolling of teams and the cries of the drivers; how he woke up and by chance found a team of his own regiment which bore him with springless axles for hours, while he slept; how he woke up to find innumerable teams awaiting their turn to move, and heard the Quarter-master say that if they didn't start to night the rebels might be upon them in the morning; how he left the team and his hard bread and handkerchief, and marched on after the regiment through mud which momentarily closed over his U. S. shoes and threatened to sink them irremediably; how he at dusk arrived at the camp of the 2nd Maine, where a good Samaritan gave him corn cake and meat and tea, but for want of accommodation suffered him to spend the night on a log in the rain; how at daylight of yesterday he reached the 19th, "played out" and wet and muddy from top to toe. * * The 2d and 3d there was a cold rain; to-day is pleasant. We are moved into a temporary camp. I have washed to-day pants, shoes and stockings, and feel clean again; I thought that a pursuit was the toughest possible experience, but a retreat beats it ten to one. Saturday, Sunday, Monday and Tuesday nights we marched or lay awake; and all day long we fought. We have been in 4 engagements, marched 25 miles, lost 176 men, and covered ourselves with glory. The Rebels have taken all our sick and wounded, and followed, perhaps driven us, to the cover of gunboats. We are at a loss to imagine whether this is strategy or defeat. Time will show. At every point we have repulsed the rebels with heavy loss, though they have taken immense stores of us, and we have destroyed much more, to save it from them. We have received large reinforcements which now hold the front and give us rest. McClellan often rides along our lines and is the idol of the men. To-day he visited us, and the long unused instruments of music played again, and cannon fired salvos. We have received a mail, the first for a week.

Good bye,   EDGAR.

GALLANT SERVICE SECURES A COMMISSION.

"The Lord is the strength of my life; of whom shall I be afraid?" Psalms XXVII. I.

On Monday, June 30, in the language of Gen. A. L. Webb, "the Union troops successfully resisted three separate attacks on flank and rear. There was no more critical day in the campaign."

One of these encounters is known as the Battle of White Oak Swamp. Capt. J. G. B. Adams of the 19th writes as follows: "Lieut. Edgar M. Newcomb was one of my best friends, and a better soldier never served in the Union Army. He was Sergeant Major during the Seven Days' Fight from Fair Oaks to Harrison's Landing. He and myself rallied the regiment after the third charge at White Oak Swamp, in which Major Howe was killed and half of the line disabled. We were selected after said battles by vote of the Officers as two of the enlisted men that had distinguished themselves, and promoted Lieutenants. As Officers we marched and fought side by side."

Capt. Stephen I. Newman fully confirms the above statement: "Newcomb was a very cool man under fire, and the field officers spoke of him as a brave soldier at the battle of White Oak Swamp, Nelson's farm." Subsequently at Malvern Hill his praiseworthy conduct was observed and mentioned by the officers."

Another fellow-soldier gives this testimony: "Newcomb's bravery was so distinguished as to be the general subject of remark among men who were accustomed to regard all dangers as so many trivial things easily forgotten when passed." As stated by the Rev. J. C. Fernald and Capt. Adams, Newcomb "was promoted to the rank of Second Lieutenant for gallant conduct while in action on the Seven Days' Retreat from Richmond."

The following paragraph was taken from a letter published in the Boston *Journal*: "The 19th in the fight of Monday, June 30, behaved with unparalleled bravery. Col. Hinks and Lieut. Col. Devereux were wounded, and Major Howe was killed; also a large number of captains and lieutenants were either killed or wounded. Notwithstanding this terrible decimation, it never wavered, never flinched; but stood to the last, and joined in that last onset which sent the rebels back to Richmond, defeated and routed."

On receiving his commission Newcomb was at first assigned to Co. K. At this time the Captain was absent wounded and the First Lieutenant was ill. Consequently our friend suddenly found himself in command of the company which always held the right of the regimental line. A member of Co. K, Mr. Charles A. Newhall, of Saugus, clerk of the Nineteenth Regiment Association, has contributed the following anecdote: "I call to mind one incident in which I was personally interested, which tends to make me remember him as a man of feeling, and kind-hearted. At one time he had command of the Co. which I was in, and I was sick, but had not been excused from duty by the Surgeon; and Lieut. Newcomb insisted that I should go on dress parade, although I told him that I did not feel able; but as we had but few men in the Co. he ordered me to go, and of course I had to obey. But after we had formed our line I was taken with a sudden faintness; and the first thing I knew after that, I was in my tent with Lieut. Newcomb leaning over me, and I never saw any one feel worse than he did, to think he had made me go on parade when I was so sick. And every day while I was sick, which was for 3 or 4 weeks, he visited me, and did all he could for me like a brother, and I have always had a great respect for him."

CAMP NEAR HARRISON'S LANDING,

JULY 15, 1862.

DEAR LEILA:

Your letter was received this morning and mother's yesterday. These are the only ones received since the news of our retreat reached home. The Scientific American comes so regularly I believe some one has kindly subscribed for it. I have also received Dailies to the 10th. We have now recovered comparatively from our fatigue, though Uncle Sam still neglects to provide tents and clothing. * * The knapsack brought from Lynnfield was left at camp, and now is the property of some Rebel. Our old camp was a mile distant from the fortifications where we lay when we received marching orders. Manning had transferred our property to the Adjutants' tent, that all might go in Head-quarters team as always heretofore. Late in the evening I heard that the Adjutant had ordered my knapsack taken down to Co. F, and obtaining permission to go to camp I found it—not. On returning the Adjutant assured me the team had carried it. It has not turned up yet. Sunday night on our forced march we were ordered to throw away every thing we could possibly spare, and away went woolen blanket and tent. Monday as we halted on the edge of the battle-field, to form for the charge to our companions' relief, orders came, 'Throw away everything,' and away went rubber blanket, overcoat and haversack. To-day I could send home all these invaluable mementoes of an enlisted man, but they are all lost, and none of my many losses have been more grievous. My pants, the same I wore home last winter and ever since, were sent home by express 3 or 4 days ago. To-day I sent to the office my sword and coat. They were declared contraband, but I hope to send them through soon.

You are doubtless anxious to know something of my new life [as a commissioned officer.] Though it is not so hard as my old one, yet I have had more than my share of work. Capt. Wass is absent wounded, Lieut. Palmer is sick, and I have been in command of the company ever since I entered; besides, I have one day done duty as Officer of the Guard, once as Adjutant, and once as Lieut. of a party at work on the fortifications. Health is good, "grub" vastly improved, leisure considerable, and the responsibility of command very pleasant. Moreover, I am now waited upon, instead of at once waiting upon myself and running on errands for others. For weeks to come we shall see no active service, and if I withstand heat and fatigue as I have done I shall live in clover. But not expecting promotion so soon, I sent most of my money home, and as Commissioned Officers don't draw U. S. rations I must send for $30 of the needful. My letters are, I suppose, common property in the family, and my orders are addressed to my banker.

Living out here is extraordinarily dear to Officers. A few of the simplest articles, such as are served to the men as rations, can be bought of the Commissary at cost, but all delicacies must be purchased at the Sutler's at an enormous price:—½ dollar cans of preserved meats and fruits, $1; cheese, 50 cents; lemons, 2 for 25 cents; raisins, 50 cents. To-day small 3-cent cakes of maple sugar were sold for 10 cents; figs are 50 cents, and ordinary molasses cakes, 2 cents apiece.

I do not think Ed. Hall experiences much warmer weather than we here. Snakes too are becoming quite frequent. Dodge, who is quite fond of reptiles, lately appeared at Head-quarters with a huge black snake. One of our men pulled an adder from his trousers-leg a few nights ago, and soon afterward a copperhead was discovered to have turned in along with two tent mates. Mosquitoes are less frequent here than at Fair Oaks, but every kind of insect abounds.

The neglect of the sick here is shameful. · An enlisted man wounded is tolerably well cared for and allowed to go home. A sick man is retained at the hospital till he recovers or dies. Exceptions are very few. An officer can be discharged or sent home only on the Surgeon's certificate that such discharge or recruiting is necessary. So we are bound to the service. If it were not so the regiments would lose many of their best officers and great numbers of men. The law seems inhuman with respect to a few, but it is in the main undoubtedly beneficial to the army.

My best regards to all inquiring friends, for I have not forgotten a single one. Putnam is probably in Richmond. The whole company speak of his bravery and coolness. Manning found a horse on the battle-field where he was seeking us, and completed the journery on horseback.

Your brother, EDGAR.

Enclosed I send you a receipt for a man who escaped from the Rebels, and with whom I was sent to the Provost Marshal, Gen. Andrew Porter. One of his staff gave me this receipt.

In the following letter Newcomb modestly discloses the cirstances leading to his promotion.

CAMP NEAR HARRISON'S LANDING,

AUGUST 2, 1862.

DEAR SISTER:

How I envy you the enjoyment of cool Malden and Mrs. Wise's house. However warm they may have seemed last summer, they are now to me the emblems of coolness and rest, as I lie sweltering under our Sibley in this lifeless climate. I have of late received letters from yourself from the beach and from Malden. You wished me to record for the benefit of "us respectable" the brave deeds which have earned me promotion and reputation for a bravery which perhaps I do not possess. I did nothing except keep cool and obey orders. I didn't get excited, and for this received Commission. The sword and coat which I entrusted to one of our discharged men were confiscated at Fortress Monroe. Fate seems to discountenance my preserving many relics. Probably they would only minister to the pride of " us," and one of that family has enough now. Many of the things I lost I have drawn again, but they are not the ones I brought from Lynnfield.

I received mother's of Sunday last Thursday. Tell her that when I get a nigger, so that I can certify on honor to having a servant, I shall draw $24.50, thus making my gross monthly receipts $105.50.

Thursday about midnight we were waked by the firing of heavy guns on the river, and at once received orders to pack knapsacks, draw rations and be ready for a march, whither no one knew. Within an hour, however, the firing had subsided, the order been countermanded, and the men turned in again. Rumors are rife that we shall soon go to Pope's reinforcement, perhaps even to Washington. Certainly we do not feel safe here. The enemy is all around us within a few miles on the opposite bank of the river; and below they line both banks. Our gunboats are our only dependence. But the fact that on these depend all our supplies, and that to run the gauntlet from Monroe (as every transport does) is an undertaking whose danger is daily increasing, makes one feel homesick. The rebels are not inactive, and if some fine day it was discovered that batteries enough lined the river to establish a blockade, cutting off our only means of supply and escape, we could not even " skedaddle."

Mother's hopes of a speedy termination of our contest are undiminished, I see, but if I return to her silver wedding it will only be as a wounded man, I fear, because we shall then be engaged in the fall campaign. But I shall visit home as soon as I can, for next January will find the war still unfinished. May I prove a false prophet.

An epistle to Leland is enclosed. Please forward. Manning was sent back to his company, but in less than 24 hours some friend procured for him a position as clerk for the Division Commissary (Gen. Sedgwick's.) Truly he is a soldier of fortune.

My love to all Malden people, especially to the Wise family.

EDGAR.

What is Webber's rank? Dodge sends this cannon cartridge-bag with his respects. I have received your needle-book. The cartridge-bag is from Yorktown.

On August 14, Newcomb was transferred from Co. K to Co. C, and the reasons for this change are given in the next letter. The march down the Peninsula, is also chronicled.

NEWPORT NEWS.

AUGUST 23, 1862.

DEAR SISTER:

You have doubtless before this learned our whereabouts from the papers, and become anious to hear from me. So I will begin with what first concerned me after my last letter. Last Thursday week Lieut. Hume returned from Richmond, having been exchanged. The Col. assigned him to Co. B; as I held his old position, 2d Lieut., Co. K, he objected and was assigned to Co. K, and I transferred to Co. C. Co. K. belonged to him rather than me; but the transfer, made without reference to my feelings, from Co. No. 1, in which I had just became acquainted, was annoying in the extreme. However I am not permanently displeased. Capt. Batchelder of '59 is a kindred spirit, and before I had been 48 hours in the company I felt more at home than when I left Co. K.

Tuesday Col. Hinks returned to command the Brigade. For several days we had been ordered to draw rations and be ready to march at a moment's notice. Friday week marching orders came, and with them that Yorktown was our destination. At 5 P. M., all was ready for the march, the men in line on parade, the baggage including knapsacks going down the river in transports. Hour after hour passed, and we spread our blankets, lay down to sleep, and waked in the morning to find ourselves still on the parade. About 9 A. M. of Saturday, we marched. Truly the country around our camp is the garden of the Peninsula. The scenery is beautiful; the foliage, fruits and herbage luxuriant. We marched a few miles and halted for the night. Next day we marched 18 miles. As we neared the Chickahominy the country became more densely wooded, but lower and more sultry. At 9 P. M. we encamped on the river bank and rested, after the hardest work I had ever done of a Sunday. As the shadows lengthened, how I thought of home. You had returned from church, and sat in the parlor, or at the table, or on the piazza of Mr. Wise, happy in peace and rest, and each other's society. I was far from all, hungry and weary, and covered with dust and sweat. Excepting the evil conscience I felt much like the prodigal son.

Early next morning we crossed the river on a pontoon stretched across its mouth, and while we rested a few hours the Captain and myself bathed. Then we marched again, and in the afternoon halted by a millpond, a cornfield and a blackberryfield. Here let me mention that, whereas on our march to Winchester the troops did no damage for which officers did not have to pay, this time we hardly passed orchard, cornfield or pig pen that was not cleaned out with impunity.

Early next morning we marched, and about noon we passed through Williamsburg, a city in time of peace containing 5002 or 6000 inhabitants, but now most of the houses are shut up, and few looked on us as we strode through their wide, sandy streets. Here is the College of William and Mary. Just outside the city are the fortifications of the the rebels, which cost us so much the 5th of May last. The woods are scarred with shot and shell, and numerous graves saddened us all, when having passed the city of the living we found ourselves almost at once in the city of the dead. But we go marching on, and at nightfall halt by a pond, or as some say, Warwick river. Wednesday we start for Yorktown, now only 10 miles distant. Through suffocating dust and under an almost tropical sun, we had struggled along and our weary constant marching had begun to tell on the men, but they thought of the transports awaiting them at Yorktown, and saw the pure water of the York at our feet. Massachusetts boys feel deeply, but they are not so demonstrative as others. Still though fatigue and discipline prevented cheering, we no sooner saw the scene and felt the cool salt breeze than a gush of joy welled up from every heart. Here we halted, and at once the river was black with human heads. Off rolled the dust in balls of thick mud, and all that alloyed our joy was returning to our wet and dirty clothes. Roast corn we had for dinner, and pork, and soft bread and tea, and then lay down at night, happy that our journey was ended. Vain delusion! About 11 we were waked up to draw rations and prepare to march at day-break to Hampton, twenty odd miles. At day-break we started, and all day long we marched. Never had the sun been hotter, or the dust thicker. Few were the halts and quick the marching. Many were sun-struck, among them Lieut. Hill. Hundreds fell out, and when at last Gen. Sedgwick concluded to halt, we filed into the field at Big Bethel. Co. C had three men of the twenty-eight that answered to morning roll-call. Most of the regiment came in a few hours later, though some did not arrive till last night. About 2 Friday A. M., we began the seventh day of our march, and at 11 reached our present camping ground at Newport News. The rain which has been so long withheld during our stay at Harrison's Landing, and so long impending during our dusty and burning march, fell in torrents during the last two miles of the march, and wet us through, so that even the refreshment of lying down after our week's work was for a while denied us, but by and by the sun came out and we rejoiced again. I had taken the precaution to stow away clean clothes in a team of extra baggage which met us here, and had the exquisite joy of feeling thoroughly renovated.

How I leaped for joy at the news that my worldly possessions were safe at home—trunk, coat, watch, commission—an accumulation of good fortune absolutely stunning. My box, however, is not at hand. It came to Harrison's Landing with many others, as we were ordered to move, and the express company returned it to Fortress Monroe. There is a possibility of my never getting it in the bustle and change which for some time will accompany our Division. The cannon cartridge bag Dodge sent you contained powder to send a rebel ball against us, when it was found in Yorktown. The enclosed paper is a legal document I picked up on the first day of our march at Charles City Court House, which had been long ago evacuated by the limbs of the law who left behind them numerous papers like this. I visited the Court House, tavern and jail.

There is much speculation about our future, and some probability of our going to North Carolina or New Orleans, but nothing definite. I shall write as often as I can, and you need not fear to address me with equal frequency, for mails come to us as surely as ever.

Your brother,   EDGAR.

In the letter dated Sept. 1, will be found particulars in regard to the passage by transport to Alexandria; then come the sad details of forced marches, covering the retreat of Pope's defeated army. At length we find Edgar defending Fairfax Court House, which he first visited in boyhood, as previously stated.

FAIRFAX COURT HOUSE,

SEPT. 1, 1862.

DEAR BROTHER:

Sunday, Aug. 24, we lay at Newport News, resting after our seven days' march. Monday at 9 A. M. we marched to the Landing and embarked on the steamship Atlantic. The roadstead was full of shipping, and in front of the Landing lay the half sunken masts of the Cumberland, the unfortunate opponent of the Merrimack. Newport News is situated on a high bluff. Below flows the James with its fine sandy beach and heaps of oysters. Four regiments of our brigade were crowded aboard the Atlantic, 100 officers in the cabin, and 2000 men wherever they could find place to stand. None knew our destination. Tuesday morning we passed Hampton Roads, Monroe with its low gray walls, and late in the afternoon we anchored at Aquia creek for orders. The next morning we proceeded up river and anchored off Alexandria, where at 4 P. M. we disembarked, and after marching three miles halted in an open field just in time to experience the full force of a shower. * * Next day at 5 P. M. we were ordered to march seventeen miles to Chain Bridge. We marched till 1 next A. M., and bivouacked till 5. Then we marched to the vicinity of the bridge and halted till noon. We then marched ten miles to Tenallytown, 6 miles from Washington. Scores of our soldiers fell by the way, from fatigue and hunger; for since leaving Harrison's Landing they had had only one ration other than coffee and hard bread.

Their strength, enfeebled by peninsular experience, was more sorely taxed than ever before. Here at last may we rest, said they, as on Saturday night they broke ranks and lay down to sleep. Soon the officers' call sounded, and we received orders to march at 2 Sunday A. M., for Manassas. Promptly we started, and in the morning twilight crossed canal bridge, passing through Georgetown. It began to rain, and again we knew Virginia mud. At 7 we halted for breakfast one-half hour, and marched till 3 P. M., when we halted in an open field in the rain. As evening came on we hoped to sleep here, but conflicting reports having come from the front, Col. Hinks posted us in line of battle and sent for orders. At 9 we marched to Fairfax. Oh, the horrors of that march. Many were barefoot, most footsore, and all stiff from uninterrupted marching. When we halted, 100 men remained of our whole regiment. We drew up in line of battle across the road, faced to the rear, for guerillas had attacked the train we passed a few hours before. To-day we rest, prepared however to repel attack and defend the two guns in front of the Court House. How much did father or mother think, when we entered Fairfax thirteen years ago, I should one day re-visit it to save it from destruction? * * After moving hither and thither till we could hardly move longer, hoping each day would bring the long-desired and promised rest, we started at midnight to cover a third retreat. To-day I have eaten and rested, but it will take weeks to recover from fatigue and privation. Rumor has it we shall go to Poolesville, and while I write Banks' column is pressing up to Harper's Ferry. The men newly-recruited are worse than useless. They cannot fight, for they are not drilled. Consequently the few old troops must do most of the duty, and wherever Jackson goes we must move to meet him.

I have heard of Mr. Stone's acceptance of the Chaplaincy of the 45th to regiment, and admire his patriotism. Our Captain's name is George W. Batchelder; 1st Lieutenant, Samuel S. Prime. I am glad to hear that you tried sleeping in the open air and found it less agreeable than you anticipated. Perhaps if you sleep without tent or rubber blanket, and in the rain, you would like it less. I am heartily glad you are resigned to your position in the home guard and fire department. Direct the box "Sumner's Corps, Sedgwick's Division, Dana's Brigade," not writing Washington or any other place.

[Extract from a letter written early in Sept., 1862.]

The fresh troops are worse than useless. They don't know how to fight, and the shadow of an enemy makes them run. No reliance whatever is put in them, and though doubtless in time they will become veterans, they are now only fit to garrison the forts about Washington. For instance, they are picketed along the road to Chain Bridge, and many troops having passed over the road during the day, some stragglers whom night had overtaken hastened on in the darkness to rejoin their regiments. The pickets immediately gave the alarm and fled. The garrison was called out in readiness to save the fort from rebel hands. Nor were the facts known till we explained them on coming up next morning. The contempt of our men for these " gingerbread soldiers " is as amusing as it is intense.

You doubtless want to know how I bore the trying times of last week. All I can say is I marched it and did not fall out. Never before was I so completely used up. But now we are near the front and we shall not retreat. We cannot go much further forward. At any moment we may be attacked, and the sound of cannon-firing is almost as constant as the rattling of baggage wagons and ambulances, which constantly pass us night and day. Since Friday we have not had six successive hours when we were not marching. Saturday A. M., we rose at 2. Sunday it rained, and after marching almost beyond human endurance we fell asleep between wet blankets. To-night it rains again, and Lee's whole left wing is reported to be marching on us. Certainly it doesn't promise rest. People say I am an exception in preserving and increasing health. Manning's constitution is impaired perhaps for life. Barrows is much weaker than a year ago, and most of my acquaintances seem to have lost somewhat of their former vigor.

We again find the 19th Mass. and another regiment assigned to the responsible, dangerous and honorable position of rear guard.

TENALLYTOWN, SEPT. 4, 1862.

Lee's whole force didn't come down upon us, though a severe rainstorm did, and we spent a quiet night on the wet ground and under wet blankets. Towards morning it was bitter cold. About 10 A. M. Tuesday, we fell back into an immense field where cavalry, artillery and infantry were huddled together. Here we passed the 38th N. Y., but though the regiment had been engaged the night before, I might not stop to see Alonzo. At the further end of the field we halted till 6 P. M., and then followed in the rear of the rearmost regiment. Before we had reached the protecting wood the enemy had planted their guns behind us, and we could readily see them protected by numerous cavalry on the very spot we had left not fifteen minutes before. Thick and fast flew the shell, bursting in front and rear, beside and over us, and we were hindered by the crowded columns before us. Three men of Co. C were hit but not hurt by spent pieces of shell. By this time we had learned that our 19th and the 1st Minnesota formed the rear guard, an honor well to be proud of. Thus we lay in the woods alongside the battery, the Minnesota a few hundred yards in front of us. Soon a terrible volley rang through the woods and Gen. Howard rode along with "get ready, boys, to repel a cavalry charge." But the Minnesota's steadiness and two shells from our battery discouraged Secesh, and we soon continued our retreat, halting again behind a fence. Reb however didn't follow any further, and we marched on. Just this side of Vienna a panic was created by a runaway horse. Some officers fired at him or into the air. Cavalry in front became frightened and swept down the road like a whirlwind, firing right and left. We heard the discharges, and seeing the masses in front rush from the road, and hearing the clattering of hoofs grow louder and louder, we imitated those in front, and in a twinkling were hid behind the trees. The 106th Pennsylvania carried us bodily by their impulse.

"THE NIGHT BEFORE THE BATTLE."

But in the tent that night, awake,
  I ask if in the fray I fall,
Can I the mystic answer make,
  When the angel sentries call?
And pray that Heaven may so ordain,
  Where'er I go, what fate be mine,
Whether in pleasure or in pain,
  I still may have the countersign.

FITZ-JAMES O'BRIEN.

The Army of the Potomac fought few battles more critical than that which for long anxious hours hung in the balance upon the banks of the sluggish Antietam. The importance of the issue was appreciated by officers and men. Each of the opposing armies prepared for a tremendous and decisive struggle. After exhausting marches and untold deprivations, rendered still more serious by stubborn preliminary conflicts in a mountainous region, the hostile forces faced each other in the vicinity of Sharpsburg. On the night of September 16, 1862, while the destiny of a nation remained undecided, and while the fate of a multitude of soldiers was obviously impending, it is not strange that the minds of the combatants were imbued with unusual solemnity. Lossing remarks that "the night of the 16th was passed by both armies with the expectation of a heavy battle in the morning. Few officers found relief from anxiety, for it was believed by many that it might be the turning point of the war. Only the Commander-in-chief of the National army seems to have had a lofty faith that all would be well. The contest was opened at dawn by Hooker with about 18,000 men."

The following incident is kindly related by Capt. William A. Hill: "On one occasion, Newcomb told me afterwards, his Captain (George W. Batchelder, another noble fellow) asked him as they were about 'turning in' for the night, on the eve of the battle of Antietam, to read a chapter aloud. Newcomb complied, and was asked to continue until he had, by the light of the bivouac fire, read several chapters; then under the same blanket they lay down to rest, Capt. Batchelder to his last sleep upon earth, for he was killed in battle on the following day; Newcomb to answer the summons in the next battle, Fredericksburg.

After Batchelder died Newcomb told me of the incident stated above, and told me how surprised he was at the Captain's request, and how happy it made him to comply. After the reading and before they slept, Batchelder, as if forewarned of the fate which he was to meet in a few hours, talked as he never had before to Newcomb, in regard to the affairs of the company; telling him among other things of certain money, the 'Company Fund,' which he had from time to time sent home to his father in Lynn for safe keeping; advising him in regard to matters pertaining to the company, and making in general such arrangements as one would make if taking leave of them forever."

In his letters to friends at home Lieut. Newcomb makes no reference to this touching scene; but Mrs. M. W. Batchelder, in the *Harvard Memorial Biographies*, acknowledges the receipt of a letter from him, containing the following passage: "After supper in the twilight of September 16, George took my Bible, and as well as I can recollect, read aloud portions of the 19th and 90th Psalms. Sweet was that evening communion: it was our last. The chief end of God's providence is to teach men; and the value of its lessons is generally according to their difficulty. How golden the knowledge, how sweet the joy we may work out from this great sorrow. We had hoped for George a glorious future. Shall it be less bright because not wrought out in our presence?"

Capt. Hill writes: "The enemy was following us closely at the time George was wounded, and we were obliged to leave him on the field in the care of James H. Heath, a young man of his company. He fainted several times while being taken to the hospital. He conversed freely and cheerfully until between 3 and 4 o'clock the same day, when he began to fail; and continued to sink rapidly till he passed quietly from the sleep of life to the sleep of death, being conscious to the last. His last words were 'My mother, oh, my mother'." His brother Charles died 8 days before (Sept. 9) of fever "brought on by being worn out at the battle of Baton Rouge. On the 5th of November, as the shades of evening were falling upon the earth, they were together laid to rest in a soldier's grave."

The death of a multitude of Union soldiers at Antietam was not in vain. President Lincoln had long been waiting for a Federal victory, and on Sept. 22, 1862, issued a proclamation declaring that the slaves of all persons in States which, on first day of January, 1863, should be in rebellion, should be thenceforth and forever free. By this noble act President Lincoln "rose to the serene heights of Zion, received light and knowledge and power from an Eternal Source, fixed by a word the moral judgment of mankind in sympathy with our national cause, secured the verdict of history and the prayers of the good in every land, and humbly awaited the favor of Almighty God."

The gallant part taken by the 19th Mass. is recorded in a letter written on the day after the battle. It will be noticed that, after Capt. Batchelder was wounded (the First Lieut. being sick) Lieut. Newcomb was in command of Co. C. during the closing hours of the eventful conflict. He does not forget to mention the gallant conduct of the men; and, as will afterward appear, his own bravery was remembered by others.

NEAR KEEDYSVILLE,

SEPT. 18, 1862.

DEAR SISTER:

My last letter was written from Hyattstown and mailed in Washington by our Sutler. Next day we marched again in three columns, the centre one passing through the town; ours, the left one, passing through the fields outside. A hot and dusty march brought us to Clarksville', I believe; near which we passed the night and proceeded toward Frederick. The railroad bridge had been burned by the rebels, though strangely enough the highway bridge across the same stream (Monocacy) remained intact. The telegraph was down the whole way along. Near Frederick we halted and formed for review. McClellan and staff rode along and halted in the city till all the troops passed him. Frederick is the largest town I have seen in Maryland, except Baltimore, having brick buildings and sidewalks, and churches and stores. As we marched down the main street the Stars and Stripes were flung from many places, and happy homelike faces beamed on us. Five days of rebel possession had disgusted them and impoverished them, so that they were glad enough to hail their deliverers. The rebels had cleaned out stores and dwellings of whatever provision they could find, paying for them, if they paid at all, in Confederate shin plasters. But as soon as we approached, the people began to cook for us, bringing out as we passed, cake, pie and bread. We halted and passed the night a mile beyond Frederick, and Sunday, [Sept. 14,] at 3 A. M., marched on. Now we began to ascend the mountains in good earnest. The roads were good, but the hills were steep enough. We heard sharp artillery firing ahead, and pressed on. As we arrived at the summit of a hill somewhat higher than the rest, commanding an extensive view of the ground in front, we saw all at once the two lines of the opposing cannon, as the white smoke rolled from their muzzles 5 or 6 miles distant. Onward we hastened and about 3 P. M., halted in a field and cooked our late dinner. At dusk we marched again to a point within two miles of the rebel pickets, and Monday morning pushed onward. At the top of the ridge is a gap where the rebels had made their stands Sunday. Here during a short halt I visited the 13th who lay on the other side the road, and saw George. He is looking finely, has had plenty of marching since he came here, and the regiment was ordered to throw away their knapsacks the night before, in immediate anticipation of a fight, but they escaped it. George did not recognize me at first. He said I had changed so. We separated when he marched on after the flying foe.

About noon we passed through Boonesboro, where a few hours before our cavalry had charged and routed rebel cavalry. Here too people gave us food and drink as we passed through Keedysville, and encamped three-quarters of a mile beyond. All day Tuesday the artillery fight lasted. McClellan with his staff rode to the top of a hill overlooking the scene, and after carefully inspecting the rebel position turned to one of his officers remarking: "Col., we shall have a severe fight here, and lose many men. They have a very strong position."

At 2 Wednesday morning [Sept. 17,] reveille sounded. Soon artillery and musketry began, and by 6 the rebels had retired one and one-half miles or so. At 7 we were ordered to Hooker's support. Over ploughed land, through cornfields we marched; through a brook kneedeep we waded. Over fences and through woods Gen'ls. Sumner, Sedgwick, Dana, Howard and Gorman accompanied us, and skirmishers in front and on the flank saw the coast clear as we advanced. After a temporary lull the rattle of musketry recommenced, and forward we went. Soon one of our men, struck by a spent ball on the cross belt, staggered back, and thinking he was wounded dropped his gun and made for the rear. As he went he looked for the wound, and finding only a bruise returned amid acclamations to his post in the front rank. We climbed a fence and entered woods again; not the woods of Chickahominy swamp with stifled air and close-tangled undergrowth in the black stagnant marsh, but a growth of large forest trees and firm ground underfoot and spreading branches above, through which played mountain air. In the woods we lay down and watched the lines in front, as they stood firing at the rebels hid in a cornfield before them. Suddenly we beheld them slowly retreat. On they came over our prostrate line, crying, "they have flanked us;" but we lay quiet, waiting for orders. [That you may understand what flanking means, remember a line of battle is composed of many regiments joining each other end to end, and extending for miles. If one regiment gives away, or leaves any distance between it and the one next to it, there is great danger to the whole line; for the enemy enters the gap, and pours a fire at once in front and rear.] Soon we perceived bullets in our rear. The order was given to retreat, and after every other regiment except the Minnesota 1st had retired, we slowly retreated, firing as we went. Again and again, and at every command of the officers we formed; but the fire was so hot, the whole field across which we retreated after leaving the wood was strewed with men. Col. Hinks was dangerously wounded; Capts. Rice,

Batchelder and Hale also. Our 1st Lieut. is sick in Hospital, and I am left in command of the Co. We retired behind a stone wall and formed, determined to stand; but orders came to retreat, and we retreated till further. The rebels dared not follow us, and after one-half hour we took our present position, still holding ground from which the foe were driven, but a short distance in rear of our original position. We now number about 200, having lost seven officers, of whom, only our Captain by death. The Captain was struck by a piece of shell, just as we rallied the last time in the open field, tearing open his leg almost from knee to ankle. In the haste of the retreat he was left behind, but so soon as we halted two men volunteered to go back after him. The rebels themselves had just left and the Captain was recovered. He had lost so much blood the surgeons deemed it imprudent to amputate, and last night he died. After a long search I found his grave this morning. Another friend had written his name on a pine slab, and a third gone in search of an embalmer. His corpse will probably soon be home. Genl's Sumner, Sedgwick, Dana, Richardson, Mansfield and others are wounded. A messenger leaves at once. I cannot finish.

EDGAR.

Remarkable and untiring industry, as well as warm affection for friends at home, prompted the writing of so long a letter immediately after a tremendous battle.

OUR HERO IS COMMISSIONED FIRST LIEUTENANT.

Newcomb's deserved promotion after the battle is chronicled by one of his comrades as follows: "At Antietam he won his rank of First Lieutenant, and to have lived through the ordeal of that day was to have come from the very jaws of death."

Capt. Stephen I. Newman also refers to Edgar's promotion "for bravery at Antietam, Md."

It was not until Oct. 13 that Edgar received the news of his advancement, the commission to date from Sept. 11.

BOLIVAR, OCT. 14, '62.

DEAR CHARLIE:

I was not intending to write again before next Sunday, but "circumstances alter cases." I was informed yesterday of my promotion to 1st Lieut., Co. C, to date from Sept. 11. The pay is only $5 per month greater, but the increased distinction and the brevity of my 2d

Lieutenancy, together with the surprise I felt at the news, make it very pleasant to me, and, I know, to you. Please send me by next mail two sets shoulder-straps (1st Lieut.'s) of the same pattern as those sewed on my coat and blouse by James & Co. Since Col. Devereux's return we have drilled very severely in battalion movements. He is the only man in the regiment now competent to handle us. No news of any importance. Our mess proceeds finely, and all hands unite in praise of the caterer and cook. Vague rumors are afloat that we are to return to Massachusetts to recruit. Every one connected with the Regiment will devote his whole influence to that end, but the result is doubtful. God grant that we may, and I for one will enjoy U. S. service as I have never before. * * But, whatever the event, remember it is all for the best, and in its own natural tendency will make us more perfect men and Christians. I am anxiously expecting my box, and if you have not sent it, direct to Harper's Ferry. The call sounds for dress parade, and I must bid you good-bye. Paymaster has not come yet.

EDGAR M. NEWCOMB,

1st Lieut. Commanding Co. C, 19th Mass. Vols.

BOLIVAR, OCT. 27, 1862.

DEAR SISTER:

Enclosed I send my shadow to you. It is not yet one half hour old and is tolerably faithful; but I am not " cockeye," and the picture, to use a comrade's phrase, " is not Newcomb." As I look at it I can remember how I looked last February, and note that 9 month's campaigning has wrought some change, whether for better or worse I dare not judge.

Since my last letter I have received the shoulder-straps and Mr. Stone's sermon. All give perfect satisfaction. I laughed as I read of your contemplated gift to my company. It has gradually swelled from 12 to 20; from 20 to 34. Yet whatever gift you send will be gladly and gratefully received.

We have our petition to go home forwarded to Washington with McClellan's endorsement, " unable at present to give it my favorable consideration." Our only hope now is to get oint Garrison or Winter Quarters, so far from the scene of active operations as to render leaves of absence once more possible.

It is getting quite cool. Officers have wall tents with stoves; but the ' poor soldiers,' shelter-tents under which they lie all night exposed to cold. Moreover, orders have been issued forbidding the issue of clothing or ammunition to Sumner's Corps at present; by which many of us are left unprovided with shirts, drawers, shoes, stockings, overcoats, or even blankets. Nor is there any means of procuring them.

Yesterday we went on picket. For the first time since we arrived at Fairfax, two months ago, it rained all day. The men without shelter or sufficient clothing suffered much from wet and cold, though not so much as before Yorktown. We may go South this winter; or into Winter Quarters in Pleasant Valley, Md., some five miles from here; or into Garrison around Baltimore or Washington. The fact that clothing is withheld (probably for troops that go forward) gives probability to either of the last two. Rumors are rife, nothing is known.

Often I dream of home by night, and my thoughts of it by day are only marred by knowing 'Father is sick. Give Webber my congratulations at having been a successful charmer, and thank him for his frequent notes. * * Manning was well the last I saw of him. Col. Devereux and Capt. Plympton, whom mother will remember, have their wives out here.

Your brother,   EDGAR.

The army of the Potomac continued its march to Falmouth, nearly opposite Fredericksburg; and items of interest will be found in Newcomb's letters.

WARRENTON, VA., Nov. 10, 1862.

DEAR BROTHER:

My last letter was written from Paris, Va., since which we have marched by easy stages and without opposition to our present camp, where we arrived yesterday. Early this morning we fell in, to see McClellan as he rode along our lines for the last time. From every quarter poured living masses of men, till both sides of the road were lined. On every hill-top were planted batteries. As he approached the regiments dipped their colors and presented arms. Immediately the salute was exchanged for three rousing cheers and salvos of artillery. The great commander wept like a child, and the great army, his creature, have shed more tears to-day than ever before during the eighteen months of their trying experience. Neither the government nor the country have any idea what a hold little Mac. has on our hearts. He may have erred, undoubtedly has, but we believe there is no one who can fill his post of duty, as there is no one who can fill his place in our hearts. Most foully has he been wronged, and the army will not be slow to resent it. * * We believe that ere long the nation will recall McClellan, but it will cost months of toil and millions of money to repair this error. If McClellan wished to establish himself Supreme Dictator to-day, the army in the heat of their resentment of this wrong would be with him.

We shall probably remain here only a few days. If you have not sent the box, add to the list one-half dozen silk handkerchiefs, a sponge in a rubber bag, and the Atlantic Monthly for October and November, and send as soon as possible. I shall probably send this by the Drum Major of our regiment. The package in paper contains my shoes which have seen all the hard service from Nelson's Farm to Antietam. The haversack and contents belong to Capt. Batchelder. Please see that they are sent to his father at Lynn.

In haste,   EDGAR.

The following descriptive letter favors us with glimpses of Edgar's poetic taste.

NEAR FALMOUTH,

NOV. 27, 1862.

DEAR SISTER:

Day before yesterday I forwarded my Corporal's and Sergeant Major's warrants, which you have doubtless received. They both need the Col.s, signature, which I shall prize all the more highly because written with his wounded arm. The warrant in my trunk is on paper, and therefore inferior to this on parchment. Charlie will doubtless preserve them in safety.

It will probably interest you to know how I spent this day. I awoke about 7 A. M. with a "bursting" headache. The day was bright and warm, though it had frozen during the night. Breakfasted on flapjacks of peculiar construction. Flour being very scarce, I had procured 5 lbs. at the rate of $20 per barrel, and mixed with a small portion an equal bulk of powdered hard tack; frying in a spider, and eating with pork fat and sugar.

Procured a pass to Falmouth, and at 9 A. M. started for the village a mile distant. A neighboring height diverted me, and I ascended it to find a battery of six Parrotts commanding the town, the river and the country beyond. Following the ridge of hills I soon came upon another battery. In fact a succession of batteries protects us now, threatens all the open country on the other side the river, and will cover our advance in the future. The left bank of the river is high, and commands Fredericksburg and the whole country around for two or more miles from the river. Every road and field and moving thing can be clearly discerned for that distance, owing to the unbroken nature of the ground and the absence of woods.

At the edge of this stretch, however, the country is well wooded, and from among the tree-tops rises the smoke of numerous rebel encampments. In one place the naked eye can discern a dark heap, which the glass reveals to be 1000 rebel troops hard at work on a heavy fortification. I continued down the river to a point opposite Fredericksburg. The Rappahannock is hardly wider than the Charles at Watertown. All along this bank lie our pickets in posts of three or four, the posts thirty paces from each other. All along the further bank, and so near that conversation is quite easy, lie the rebel pickets. Almost within stone's throw of each other pace the sentries of the two armies, ready to give the alarm at any hostile demonstration.

Falmouth on the left bank is a small village with two or three churches. Fredericksburg, on the right bank a mile below, is the second city of Virginia, with seven churches. We see the sentries as they pace the streets leading down to the river; and men, women and children as they cross them on their different errands; we hear the blacksmith at work in his shop, and the rattle of vehicles in the streets; but the bridges are all gone, the ferry boat locked on the other side, and the river separates us from —— something. As I stood upon the heights looking down into the city, I wished I had all the inmates of fifty-six [Worcester street, Boston] to look with me. Could this be war? The peaceful city, beautiful country and quiet river, even the smoke of the camp and picket fires curling slowly upward, betoken no strife. The few white tents in sight look innocent enough. The sunlight plays with the sentry's bayonet, and even the frowning cannon seem but as the shade necessary to perfect the picture. Perhaps it is all a delightful dream, and I wished again that all at home might see and enjoy.

But the quiet is only seeming, and before to-morrow morning 300,000 men may be struggling for the mastery, and river and city and country become the hospital and grave of the children of strife. We wait here only till the railroad is finished, so that transportation shall not fail us. This land is given over to Secessia; and its inhabitants, who gave liberally to rebels, either refuse to sell, or demand enormous prices for provisions. This morning I paid twenty-five cents for a head of cabbage.

Returning home I dined on fried liver and mackerel, which my cook found by chance, and potatoes. Our mess is dissolved by mutual agreement till we go again into camp, but that I might not feed alone, I invited a fellow-officer to dine with me, and we dined, thinking, however, of home all the time. Next year may we be together again.

* * Just eaten supper, fritters of hard tack. When I come home I shall cook several camp-dishes if you *all* agree to *eat* them with me. Hard tack and pork alone, with sugar and salt to flavor, can be made into six different dishes. It will not cost me much to live when I get home; and if father forbids the house, I can take my blanket and tent, pitch the latter in the street before fifty-six, and lay me down to sleep with a clear conscience and a good digestion. Charlie may sleep with me, if he will bring the wood and water. A tin plate and dipper will form my cooking kit, and a dollar's worth of hard tack will last us a month.

But we cannot always realize our schemes of Utopia, and I will go no further. Mother's letter of Nov. 9 I have not received, and suppose it is lost. Yours written in Park street vestry is at hand. In your next send me some stamps. A copy of the Lynn Reporter, Nov. 15, has reached me. Love to all.

EDGAR.

NEAR FALMOUTH,
NOV. 27, 1862.

DEAR BRO.:

Yours of —— reached me, and I was highly pleased with its enthusiastic spirit. At the first, I was about to return an unconditional refusal. I wanted you much, but the bivouac and the battlefield are not places for a civilian. Later I decided to send for you, but knowing that it was next to impossible for any one not in the U. S. service to reach us, that part of the way was so infested with guerrillas that Capt. Merritt still lingers at Washington; and that before you could possibly reach us we expect to be across the river and pursuing the enemy by longer marches than you could make in pursuit of us; I finally decided to wait a few weeks till we can see how things are to work. If we (or only I) return, I don't want you here now. If we flee before Johnny, I don't want you any way. But if we are to campaign this winter, or to go into winter quarters here, you shall visit me; and if there is any probability of our entering Richmond, you shall enter with the 19th. The expense now of coming here and returning would be about $50, and if we moved while you are coming, infinitely more. But so soon as the railroad is completed, and the first rush of transportation over, and the impending battle in this quarter fought, I shall be most happy to give you a soldier's entertainment.

Now content yourself till after New Year's at farthest, and I will try to accommodate you.

EDGAR.

The Rev. James C. Fernald contributes a pleasant paragraph written by Capt. John C. Chadwick: "Some of my most profitable hours have I spent in his [Newcomb's] company while in our tent, or log house, after the day's duties were done. These were the hours in which he delighted to speak of his *beautiful home,* as he termed it, as well as of the temptations of camp-life and the regard he felt for the spiritual welfare of brother officers and fellow soldiers." At this time Capt. Chadwick was in command of Co. C.

A PROVIDENTIAL PILGRIMAGE.

NEAR FALMOUTH,
Nov. 30, 1862.

DEAR BROTHER:

Col. Devereux is ordered to have his men log their tents, and therefore I infer a longer stay here than was at first expected. I should be most happy to have you visit me before Christmas. Therefore, if you wish to come, take the cars at B. & W. R. R. Depot, Monday, Dec. 8, at 8 A. M., buying a through ticket to Washington, where you will arrive Tuesday morning, Dodd's Express conveying you through N. Y. At the Provost Marshal's office, corner I and 19th streets, Washington, you will procure a pass to the 19th Regiment at Falmouth. At 8 A. M., boat leaves foot of 6th street (where you arrive by horse railroad) for Aquia creek, where you take rail to Falmouth, U. S., furnishing transportation from W. to F. Before you leave, see if Harnden & Co. will soon send my box up. Come Monday, or at any rate Tuesday. * * Now don't encumber yourself with baggage. Send word Saturday, if you start Monday. I will meet you if I can; if not, find first Howard's Division, Couch's Corps; then Hall's Brigade (formerly Dana's); then the 19th Mass. Remember brass and patience eventually succeed, but you will have a hard time to find me. Better go to the Provost Marshal's office at Falmouth and inquire the way to the corps and division. If I am not at home use my tent till I come. Don't forget to dress warm. You have now all the help I can give you this side of Falmouth. May we meet before long.

EDGAR.

The importance of this visit will appear on a subsequent page.

NEAR FALMOUTH,
NOV. 30, 1862.

DEAR FATHER:

I did not expect to write again so soon when I last wrote, but circumstances alter, and man is the creature of circumstance. We shall remain here for some weeks, and as we must work this winter, I shall probably be unable to come home. I have sent for Charlie to come and visit me, hoping at once to enjoy his society, to benefit his health, and to give him some idea of a soldier's life. Believe me, a week or two of our experience will not strengthen his love of camping out, though it will greatly improve his health. He cannot visit us under more favorable circumstances. The weather is tolerably mild; the camp is well located. While he can see rebeldom and an army in the field, he will be perfectly safe from harm. * * How long he will stay depends, but unless you wish otherwise he will be home before Christmas, *if he comes immediately.* I received this morning your letter enclosing $10, for which thanks. I wish I had you all here, but as that is impossible, lend me for a while my brother. We are quite busy. Inspections, Division, Brigade and Regimental drills, occupy us. The regiment is now on the bayonet exercise which we began last winter. Charlie will be a good hand to forage for " spuds " (potatoes) and hoe cakes, and if time passes heavily we can drill him. No more to-night. It is after taps when all lights should be out, and I am Officer of the Guard to-morrow, and will have to keep awake all night. Charlie must wear his watch.

EDGAR.

The following letter contains a loyal request in regard to "a most precious treasure." It is needless to add that the sacred memento has been carefully guarded. Concerning the army letters and their contents Edgar's sister writes: "I prize them more than most anything else among my possessions." These words were penned more than twenty years after her brother, the gallant christian soldier, had entered the shining ranks of the Heavenly host.

NEAR FALMOUTH,
DEC. 7, 1862.

Again, dearest sister, do I write with pencil, but only because Captain is gone and Eddie doesn't know where to find the ink. We still remain in camp, and as you learn by the daily paper more news than I can tell you, I will go on to relate what there may be of interest in my own unpublished history.

I am growing very fat, so fat that I am actually lazy; and climbing a steep hill or chopping wood puts me out of breath. I weigh 162 without overcoat. Our tent is now logged to the eaves, and yesterday we (I included) built a fire-place two and one-half feet square in the side, of sticks lined with rocks and mud, plastered chimney of course outside, like all Virginia chimneys. It is as cold here as it was last winter when I was at home, and we only keep warm by thinking how much colder is Johnny Reb without coat, blanket or shoes—a barbarous way of warming oneself, but quite successful. Not long ago we went on picket, and I slept in a kind of storehouse built of rails and cornstalks, and floored with the same. It was delicious after months of sleeping on the ground.

You were undoubtedly surprised at my sending for Charlie, but I knew it would do him good, and longed to share with him for a few weeks my luxuries. What an old man I shall be on my return; how sated with all the pleasures of this life. I had not then seen Burnside's order prohibiting all civilians from coming here without passes; but if Charles has started, as I hope he has, he cannot fail to see me with his ordinary perseverance. He will see the President sooner. If I knew his address at Washington, I might send him a pass from Sumner. But if by some mischance he should fail to reach me, the visit and the sights of Washington will ample repay him for his time, trouble, disappointment and expense. If he succeeds, two weeks of camping out will probably loose the charm of being a soldier from his bright fancy. I wish I could have you all here, but I reckon that besides extra tents and blankets we should need an extra physician.

I received a letter from Mrs. Batchelder not long ago, mentioning your visit and inquiring after George's sword, &c. I answered her at once; among other things, that the sword blade returned was his, and that he received all the attention I should ask for my own brother under such circumstances. Letters from yourself, Mother and Webber have been duly received. I enclose a letter written by one " Edward," as also the envelope. It was neither written nor directed to me, yet the reading of it, according to a way they have in the army with other people's letters, gave me much gratification.

My box is still in Washington. Perhaps I shall get it by Christmas. I return that beautiful poem on our flag. Keep it for me. Have you seen the flags? If not, go at once to the State House, and in Gen. Schouler's office you will see them. Then imagine me with waving sword and lusty voice, making myself hoarse in the cause of Victory; and with some exaggeration you have Newcomb as he appeared, &c.

One of our men has just given me a piece of the tattered flag which he picked up at the Antietam. Keep it, for it is a most precious treasure. 'Tis our State flag. Lieut. Hinks sends his regards. Capt. Merritt is still in Washington. * * The pants I put on about the 1st of Sept. are worn out. Hereafter till we reach at least a place of rest, I shall wear the pants of enlisted men.

I have spent the day reading the Bible, newspapers and army regulations, and thinking of home. And now my powers wane and I bid you good night, my own precious Leila.

Tell Mrs. Batchelder that the man who helped George from the field was Benjamin Falls.

THE BATTLE OF FREDERICKSBURG.

"And they shall be as when a standard-bearer fainteth." Isiah X. 18.
"We shall but die.". 2 Kings. VII. 4.
"For me to live is Christ, and to die is gain." Philippians I. 21.
"In the midst of life we are in death." Burial service.

We have seen that the Army of the Potomac, under General Burnside, was encamped near the Rappahannock. On the opposite bank of the river was the Army of Northern Virginia, commanded by General Lee. Years after the battle James D. Blackwell composed the appropriate stanzas given below:

Bright river! How oft has thy swift-gliding wave
Drank deep of the blood of the true and the brave;
And thy banks, fringed with woodlands, re-echoed afar
The tread of vast legions, the thunders of war.
But the combat is ended, the storm hath passed o'er,
And thy waters with life-blood are crimsoned no more;
But long shall their murmurs in memory tell
Of the heroes who fought, and the martyrs who fell.

On his arrival at Falmouth the Union commander considered a further advance impossible until the railroad in his rear was repaired. He was also delayed by the absence of pontoons, until the Confederate forces had strongly fortified the heights beyond Fredericksburg. Meanwhile the cry of the nation, "On to Richmond," was continually ringing in his ears, and he determined to make a desperate effort. At length the pontoons were brought to the brink of the river long before daybreak on Thursday, December 11, more than three weeks after Sumner's Corps reached Falmouth. "Two signal shots broke the stillness which reigned through the Confederate lines. These were the signal for Longstreet's Corps to concentrate upon the threatened point."

> Listen! Again the shrill-lipped bugles blow,
> Where the swift currents of the river flow
> Past Fredericksburg: far off the heavens are red
> With sudden conflagration: on yon height,
> Linstock in hand, the gunners hold their breath:
> A signal-rocket pierces the dense night,
> Flings its spent stars upon the town beneath:
> Hark!—the artillery massing on the right;
> Hark!—the black squadrons wheeling down to death!
>
> THOMAS BAILEY ALDRICH.

The war correspondent of the New York Herald gives a graphic account as follows:

"Last night (10th) at sundown the movement commenced. Batteries hastened to the front, wagon trains were removed from the vicinity of the anticipated battle, the ponderous pontoons hurried river-ward, and night closed down upon us bright and beautiful. Artillery never seemed to rumble so noisily before, and the sharp cluck of the iron axles echoed far and near. Down by the river everything was as quiet as peace. The river swept smoothly by, and just over there, so close one almost wished to tell them of their error, stood the rebel sentries. Silence settled down upon the town, broken only by the tones of the clock telling the midnight hours. The moon climbed higher up and the falling dew whitened into frost. At two o'clock our pickets were withdrawn, and at three the pontoon train drove down to the water. Lumber was noiselessly piled upon the ground, and the huge boats slid from off the trucks. Then we hear a splashing in the river, a dark pathway lengthens out upon the silver surface; shadows flit here and there along its track; lusty blows of hammers re-echo from side to side. And yet no sound comes from the enemy. Have they evacuated the place? Are we not to fight here after all? Suddenly, Crack! crack! crack! from a hundred muskets tells us the ball is opened. A cry of pain comes up the bank from the engineers; mules dash off with pontoons thundering after. The whiz of bullets becomes more frequent. Suddenly, boom! goes a gun; another and another, until thirty pieces are pouring shot and shell upon the devoted city. Musketry is lost to the ear in the mighty roar that re-echoes again and again from hill to hill. Gradually the fire slackens, and the engineers again attempt the completion of the bridge, but in vain, and after the third trial they fall back, bearing in their arms the wounded, dead and dying. By this time it was sunrise, the wounded began to crowd the floors of the Lacy House; and the surgeons soon had work enough.

About eight o'clock the artillery fire ceased. The fog was so dense that objects were invisible one hundred yards away from the guns. Fredericksburg was as silent as before. Again the engineers advance, and again the enemy drive them back. Orderlies gallop to the different batteries with instructions. A message orders from Aquia a spacial train with solid shot, and the thunder breaks out anew. For a time the roar is indescribably awful. The city from its walls of brick hurls back a thousand echoes which beat up against the Falmouth bluff, roll back again beyond the town, and then from distant hills once more swell over to us, as though the heavens were rent asunder. At General Sumner's head-quarters it becomes difficult to converse in a low tone, while at the batteries, orders must be signalled. By-and-by the fire ceases and one is almost awe-struck with the profound silence. The mist still clings to the river, the sun struggling up red and fiery, and the air is suffocating with the odor of gunpowder. Presently the bank of fog begins to lift a little; the glistening roofs gleam faintly through the veil; then the sunbeams scatter the clouds that intervene, and Fredericksburg, utterly desolate, stands out before us. A huge column of dense black smoke towers above the livid flames, that leap and hiss and crackle, licking up the snow upon the roofs with lambent tongues. The guns renew their roar, and we see the solid shot plunge through the masonry as though it were pasteboard. Other buildings are fired, and before sundown a score of houses are in ashes, while not one seems to have escaped the pitiless storm of iron.''

The scenes of that eventful day are also vividly portrayed by a correspondent of the New York Times:

'' At ten o'clock General Burnside gives the order, ' Concentrat the fire of all your guns on the city and batter it down.' You may believe they were not long to obey. The Artillery on the right—eight batteries—was commanded by Colonel Hays; Colonel Tompkins, right centre—seven batteries; Colonel De Russy, left—nine batteries. In a few moments a total of one hundred and seventy-nine guns on Stafford Heights, [other accounts say one hundred and forty-seven guns] ranging from ten-pounder Parrotts to four and a half inch siege guns, posted along the convex side of the arc of the circle formed by the bend of the river and land opposite Fredericksburg, opened on the doomed city. The effect was, of course, terrific, and, regarded merely as a phenomenon, was among the most awfully grand conceivable. Perhaps what will give you the liveliest idea of its effect is a succession, absolutely without intermission, of the very longest peals. It lasted thus for upward of an hour, fifty rounds being fired from each gun, and I know not how many tons of iron were thrown into the town.

The congregated generals were transfixed. Mingled satisfaction and awe was upon every face. But what was tantalizing was that, though a great deal could be heard, nothing could be seen, the city being still enveloped in fog and mist. Only a denser pillar of smoke, showing itself on the background of the fog, indicating that the town had been fired by our shells. Another and another column showed itself, and we presently saw that at least a dozen houses must be on fire.

Toward noon the curtain rolled up, and we saw that it was indeed so. Fredericksburg was in a conflagration. Tremendous though this firing had been, and terrific though its effect was on the town, it had not accomplished the object intended. It was found by our gunners almost impossible to obtain a sufficient depression of their pieces to shell the front part of the city, and the rebel sharp-shooters were still comparatively safe behind the thick stone walls of the houses.

During the thick of the bombardment a fresh attempt had been made to complete the bridge. It failed, and [as General Hunt suggested] nothing could be done till a party could be thrown over, to clean out the rebels and cover the bridge-head. For this mission General Burnside called for volunteers, and Colonel Hall of Fort Sumter fame, immediately responded that he had a Brigade (3d Brigade, 2d Div., 2d Army Corps) that would do the business. [Colonel Norman J. Hall was a graduate of West Point, and entered the service as Second Lieutenant of Artillery. After the capture of Fort Sumter he was assigned to the command of the 7th Michigan infantry. He died in 1866, and is buried at West Point. During the battle of Fredericksburg, the other regiments of his Brigade were the 19th and 20th Mass., 42d and 59th N. Y.] Accordingly the 7th Michigan and 19th Massachusetts, two small Regiments numbering in all about four hundred men, were selected for the purpose. The plan was that they should take the pontoon boats of the first bridge, of which there were ten lying on the bank of the river, waiting to be added to the half-finished bridge, cross over in them, and landing, drive out the rebels. Nothing could be more admirable or more gallant than the execution of this daring feat. Rushing down the steep bank of the river, the party found temporary shelter behind the pontoon boats lying scattered on the bank, and behind the piles of planking destined for the covering of the bridge, behind rocks, &c. In this situation they acted some fifteen or twenty minutes as sharp-shooters, they and the rebels observing each other. In the meantime new and vigorous artillery firing was commenced on our part, and just as soon as this was fairly developed, our sharp-shooters rose from their crouching places, rushed for the pontoon boats and, pushing them into the water, rapidly filled them with twenty-five or thirty each.

The first boat pushes off. Now, if ever, is the rebels' opportunity. Crack! crack! crack! from fifty lurking places go rebel shots at the brave fellows, who, stooping low in the boat, seek to avoid the fire. The murderous work was well done. Lustily, however, pull the oarsmen; and presently, having passed the middle of the stream, the boat and its gallant freight come under cover of the opposite bluffs.

Another boat follows. Nothing could be more amusing in its way than the result. Instantly we see a new turn of affairs. The rebels pop up by the hundred, like so many rats, from every cellar, rifle-pit and stone wall, and scamper off up the streets of the town. With all their fleetness, however, many of them were much too slow. With incredible rapidity the Michigan and Massachusetts boys sweep up the hill, making a rush for the lurking places occupied by the rebels, and, gaining them, each man capturing his two or three prisoners. The pontoon boats on their return took over more than one hundred of these fellows.

You can imagine with what intense interest the crossing of the first boat-load of our men was watched by the numerous spectators on the shore, and with what enthusiastic shouts their landing on the opposite side was greeted. It was an authentic piece of human heroism, which moves men as nothing else can. The problem was solved. This flash of bravery had done what scores of batteries and tons of metal had failed to accomplish. The country will not forget that little band."

By the kindness of Harper & Brothers, of New York, a view of the forlorn hope crossing the river is taken from Harper's

Weekly. The Confederate force which so long prevented the advance consisted chiefly of Barksdale's Mississippi troops, who first met the 19th Mass. at Balls Bluff and Edward's Ferry.

We have already seen that Edgar, previous to the battle and when no immediate conflict was anticipated, had sent for his brother. Charles left home at the appointed time, and arrived at Aquia Creek at dusk on Dec. 11. Hearing the heavy bombardment he hastened forward as rapidly as possible, and reached Falmouth about 6 P. M. The city of Fredericksburg was then afire in three places, and men were transporting the wounded across the river to the Lacy house and other hospitals. At this time a surgeon was probing the wound of a member of the Mass. 19th. Seven men were wounded in one of the boats while crossing, and many others fell during the sharp fight in the streets of Fredericksburg. Fearing that his brother might be wounded, Charlie (though only seventeen years of age) commenced a tour of inspection among the hospitals on the Falmouth side. When weary, he lay down beside the bivouac fire and slept till Friday morning. At an early hour of that beautiful December day, he crossed the pontoon bridge and soon found the 19th Mass. The affectionate greetings of the brothers may be left to imagination. Edgar said that his line had occupied a street, but after dark fell back near the river. Throughout the day on Friday the troops were drawn up in line of battle. There were three lines in the city. Edgar's company was in one of the houses, a portion of the time. A platoon would load in the back parlor, and then enter the front parlor to shoot at Confederates across the street. Occasionally a few shells were thrown into the city. By and by the soldiers were ordered to stack arms, and they amused themselves in searching the old houses in an orderly manner, but pillaging was strictly forbidden. Toward evening Charlie received permission to forage in the pantry of one of the houses. The flour which he delivered to the cook contained plaster of Paris, and the griddle cakes were consequently dangerous diet. On Friday night the brothers slept in the parlor of a house on Caroline street, sharing the same blanket on the floor. Edgar talked of home, and became very sad. Finally he remarked,

"After all, Charlie, you may have come to take care of me and take me home." Soon after this, at a late hour they fell asleep. During the long conversation that evening, no light was allowed, lest it should draw the rebel fire.

Early on the morning of Saturday, Dec. 13, Charlie was aroused by the order, "Fall in, Co. C." He called Edgar, who took command, and the company fell in along the sidewalk in front of the house. The men remained in line two or three hours after sunrise, when they were dismissed for breakfast. Edgar then requested his brother to go after the Christmas box which was at Potomac Creek. The patriotic young civilian, with true soldierly spirit, desired to take a musket and fall into the ranks of the color company, for he was well drilled. Edgar, anxious to keep the zealous youth out of danger, persuaded him to go after the box; saying, "Charlie, you will see fighting enough before you go away." Without further opposition the latter proceeded on his journey to Potomac Creek. Lieut. Newcomb was now at leisure for a short time, before his regiment was ordered into line of battle. A part of this precious interval was occupied in writing the following beautiful letter, [the best that he ever wrote] which was found in his pocket after he was wounded :

FREDERICKSBURG,
DEC. 13, 1862.

DEAR SISTER:

We occupied the city about 4 P. M. of the 11th, after bombarding it for almost twelve hours. The 7th Michigan of our Brigade crossed first, followed by the 19th [Mass.] Co. C first. We occupied the houses and fired from windows, from behind barns, &c., driving the enemy almost out of the city. Yesterday Charlie came over and met me, just as we had returned from picket. Our meeting was exceedingly happy. The rebels are now shelling us about half a mile below, and expecting the mail to start, and our marching orders to be given every moment, I have first written what you would be most anxious to hear. I shall now continue my story from 4 A. M. of the 11th, as well as possible.

At that time we awoke and struck our tents, just logged and furnished with fireplaces to render winter tolerable. At 6½ we marched three or four miles to the ferry, a point opposite Fredericks-

burg where the river is narrowest. Though we were the last reg't
of the Brigade and Division on the march, the latter had no sooner
halted than we passed them, all except the 7th Mich., and formed in
line on the bluff overlooking the river. Col. D. remained in camp,
his boils not permitting him to walk or ride; otherwise we flatter
ourselves we would have been the first. Didn't we feel proud as we
moved along past the regiments who looked on us with a kind of awe,
and whispered "the 19th Mass." The 7th deployed as skirmishers
on our left, and then the 19th deploying we moved forward over the
prostrate forms of another regiment, the previous advance guard, and
lay down on the river's brink to punish the sharp-shooters, who,
posted in the houses opposite, had prevented the finishing of a pontoon a few hours before. Meanwhile, the batteries above us kept up
a vigorous fire on the buildings, but neither by shot or shell did
Johnny reply. At noon the pontoon corps endeavored to finish the
bridge, but the sharp-shooters proved too many for them, and again
they retired. Soon after we were called up the bank though the
shelling continued. The city was now afire in half a dozen places.
Rarely was a sign of life visible, though we knew that among the
buildings were hid perhaps thousands. Amid the clouds of smoke
rose the church spires, and the only clock still counted the fleeting
hours, 12, 1, 2, and then was silent. We began to fear we should not
cross that day, though the order of the march (the 19th was second)
and all necessary directions had been issued for several hours. At 3
P. M. we were ordered again to the bank, and lay down in the cold
mud. Being still fastidious where I lay, I did not at once lie down,
but a shot from across the river whizzing by considerably accelerated
my descent. Bye and bye the pontooniers came down in fear and
trembling and began to work. During all of our terrific shelling, and
even when we fired at every head, the Rebels had kept almost
unbroken silence, but no sooner did the engineers again tackle the
boats than scores of balls warned them to desist. Our firing could
not silence them. The most violent shelling, tearing their shelters
and crashing over, beneath, and all around could not move them.
Pontooniers halted, desisted, and finally ran. Then the 7th took the
boats and piled into them, twenty in a boat, and without a moment's
delay poled over the river, amid a hail of bullets and the cheers of
thousands of soldiers who crowded the bluff. Never in my life did I
feel as I did when the first boat grounded on the opposite shore, and
its noble crew leaped out and climbed the bank, while Johnny
skedaddled down town. Alas, the first man who landed fell in the

street, mortally wounded. Now came our turn, and Co. C rushed down and crossed. Only one of our company was wounded, and he slightly in the foot. The Michiganders had captured a score of Johnnies and were marching them down as we landed. Immediately we deployed as skirmishers, and climbing the fences and filing through back gardens entered the houses on Caroline street. Everything lay in confusion, but we must skirmish, not pillage. The large white house which we occupied till fifteen minutes ago fell to my lot, and with a dozen men, entered. Up went the windows. The blinds were thrown open, the first door smashed into fragments and men posted up stairs and down. Right opposite us behind a fence lay the sharp-shooters, and soon our shots found their hiding place. We fought till dark and picketed during the night hours, and the gray-backs not so far from us as 50 from Shawmut Av. This morning the Captain counted the holes in one of the rooms of our house. Through a space 4 ft. by 4 we had sent five shot or shell, and the rebels seventy-two bullets. The pontoon was soon finished, but the Gen. probably fearing a repulse sent over only a few regiments after us, and we lay all night long at the mercy of the Rebels, had they known our weakness, but morning came and they had not troubled us. We were relieved and the picket advanced so that now, as a second or third line, we hold the houses we first held as skirmishers. All day yesterday we rested in the ruined houses, or along the desolate but crowded street. Thursday evening after Fredericksburg was taken, they shelled us, and occasionally yesterday, in which case we retired behind the buildings.

We had just been relieved from picket when Charlie came up and was introduced by Capt. Chadwick. He had been detained in Washington longer than he expected, only getting away as Surgeon's boy. He arrived opposite Fredericksburg Thursday evening after the fight, heard I was wounded and spent many hours in search of me in the hospitals; though the cases he saw were slight and few, yet his initiation to a soldier's life and a soldier's chances shocked him not a little. He spent the day with me, and after a little instruction in the customs of camp, proved himself abundantly able to provide for himself and me too. He ate little yesterday; even beef's heart, which I consider a luxury, he put in his haversack " to eat by and by." He spent half the night at a fire trying to warm himself, and this though we were in a house, and lay on a bed, and the weather was quite mild, But we laugh good-naturedly, and wait till hunger and want of sleep break him in to a soldier's life.

To-day he has gone over the river to the next station where he left my box and his valise, and if he gets back in time will tell you his experiences and give the details more fully than I.

I cannot be too grateful for the loan of Bro. Charlie, and though he came out most anxious to see a fight, my advice and orders which have been most materially strengthened by a few shells which the Rebs fired at us yesterday, will keep him out of harm's way. I am glad too that you do not limit his stay. We are on the eve of important movements, and he will have advantages which he will never regret, and can never again have, of seeing all sides of our rough life except, I hope, defeat. Then the pleasure of his society and the assurances of his care in case of an accident are invaluable.

This morning I received yours and mother's of the 7th and a paper. The shells are flying thicker and the musketry growing momentarily sharper and more continued. I hope not to be called out again, but God disposes, and we know not what an hour may bring forth. Charlie says he thinks I owe my past safety to the prayers of my friends. I have often thought the same, and when I consider the temptations of of this most trying life, my protection from sin is more marvelous than from wounds or death.

Good bye,   EDGAR.

At this time the Union lines were divided into three Grand Divisions. On Friday, Dec. 12, the larger part of the Army of the Potomac crossed the pontoon bridges, and Hall's Brigade (in the Right Grand Division) was posted in the city of Fredericksburg. The left Grand Division was stationed below the town, and the Centre was to be left in reserve during the first attack. Meanwhile, the Confederate troops prepared for resistance to the last. Their position was naturally a strong one, and the heights south of Fredericksburg had been fortified with consummate skill. In the open field the two armies were about equally matched. Behind works of immense strength General Lee had good reason to expect an easy victory. The night of the 12th was intensely cold, and the pickets on both sides suffered greatly. On Saturday morning the sun rose clear, but a dense fog enveloped the town. Opposite this point, on the Confederate left, General Longstreet was in command. On his right were the Divisions of Jackson and A. P. Hill, the entire length of the Confederate lines being nearly six miles. Historians on both sides agree as to the general features of the battle, and no extended account can be given in this brief sketch. There has been considerable discussion as to the true meaning of an order sent by General Burnside to General Franklin, who commanded the Left Grand Division of the Union army. This ambiguity was unfortunate at the outset. In accordance with the supposed intent of the Commander-in-Chief, an attack was made by General Meade (afterwards the hero of Gettysburg) about 10 A. M. So impetuous was the assault that Meade succeeded in driving a thin wedge between two of Hill's Brigades, and had he been properly supported there is a possibility that the Federal troops might have won a victory. But the force at hand was too weak, and Meade's column retired in disorder with a loss of forty per cent. Repeated charges during the day were likewise unsuccessful. A part of the Right Grand Division, under General Sumner, was ordered into action. In his front the plain was narrow, and obstructed by a canal and fences. Only a portion of his force could be employed at once. General Howard's Division (to which was attached Hall's Brigade, including the Mass. 19th) at first received instructions to make a demonstration on the Confederate left flank; but before this movement could be carried into execution, Howard was ordered to support Hancock in a desperate attempt "to carry by storm the enemy's works." Eye witnesses mention the "great gaps" ploughed through the ranks by artillery fire. They tell us how the "heads of columns in front of Marye's Heights melted away before a solid wall of fire, delivered from ranks four deep, like a snow-bank before a jet of steam." The slaughter in front of the stone wall and road cut out of the hill-side was too dreadful for description, and words are unequal to the task.

Suddenly flashed a sheet of flame
From hidden wall and from ambuscade ;
A moment more—they say this is fame—
A thousand dead men on the grass were laid.

Our soldiers who took part in the hopeless charges "met a solid sheet of lead winged with flame, poured in their faces from the sunken road." In front of the Heights our men were overpowered by " a torrent of shot and shell, grape and canister, with whistling bullets thick as hailstones." Pollard, one of the best Southern military writers, remarks that "in this part of the field the enemy displayed a devotion that is remarkable in history." Colonel Walter H. Taylor, of General Lee's staff, referring to the repulse of the Federal lines, generously observed that "their allotted task exceeded human endeavor; no shame to them that, after such courageous and brilliant conduct, their efforts lacked success."

General Burnside's official report of his losses may assist the reader to form some conception of the wholesale slaughter: " Killed, 1180; wounded, 9028; missing, 2145." The Right . Grand Division suffered much more than either of the others.

> Eighteen hundred and sixty-two,—
>   That is the number of wounded men
> Who, if the telegraph's tale be true,
>   Reached Washington City but yester e'en.
>
> And it's but a handful, telegrams add,
>   To those that are coming by boats and cars ;
> Weary and wounded, dying and sad,
>   Covered, but only in front, with scars.
>
> Orders arrived, and the river they crossed ;
>   Built the bridge in the enemy's face ;
> No matter how many were shot and lost,
>   And floated, sad corpses, away from the place.
>
> Orders they heard, and they scaled the height,
>   Climbing right into the jaws of death ;
> Each man grasping his rifle-piece tight.
>   Scarcely pausing to draw his breath.
>
>   W. F. W.

Lieut. Newcomb's heroism in this fearfully-fatal struggle is still fresh in the memory of his comrades, who have kindly contributed numerous written statements from which the following extracts are taken. Col. John C. Chadwick, now military instructor at the Mass. Institute of Technology, thus tells the story: "I went out as Adjutant of the 19th Reg't, Mass. Vols., and was then made Captain, and assigned to the command of 'C Co.,' which was the Color company. Edgar M. Newcomb was my First Lieutenant, and was serving in that capacity under my command, when he was wounded at Fredericksburg; and Sergeant Wallace T. George, of Haverhill (my First Sergeant), aided me in bringing him off the field, after I had got my company in a place of comparative safety. He was sent on a stretcher to the Lacy House Hospital, where he died.

Major H. G. O. Weymouth [who for many years has held a responsible position at the Boston Custom House] led the regiment at the battle of Fredericksburg. Col. E. W. Hinks was at home wounded. Lieut. Col. Devereux was incapacitated for duty, by a very large and angry abscess on the inside of the calf of the leg, which prevented his riding, and also walking. Major Howe was dead. Capt. Wass was at home wounded in the foot, and I think Capt. Rice was also wounded; which caused the command to devolve on Capt. Weymouth.

The regiment made three charges at Fredericksburg, and Lieut. Newcomb fell on the third charge, while advancing with the National flag in his hands. The Color Sergeants had both been shot down, and as soon as they fell, the Colors were caught up by others, who in turn were shot; and so on, until we had eleven men shot (killed or wounded) under our Regimental Colors—the National and State flags.

At last the two men holding those flags dropped, and Edgar picked them both up, and advanced, calling upon the men to follow him; when some one said, 'Newcomb, give me one of those flags;' when he handed him the State flag, retaining the National flag, under which he soon dropped.

He was struck by a Minnie bullet (I think) below the knees, shattering the bones of both legs, at about 3 or 4 o'clock, as near as I can tell now, without consulting records. We had passed down the principal street of the town, and after passing beyond its limits we filed to the right of the Pike, and then formed line to the left, under the edge of the Plateau, over which we advanced to the first, second and third charges. The 20th Mass. and 7th Michigan Regt's were with us. When we found we could not carry the works by assault, after the third charge, those two regiments fell back below the Plateau; but we, being nearer the Pike, obliqued to the left and got behind fences of yards in the rear of some houses fronting on the Pike.

After Newcomb dropped, and while getting my company in

a place of safety, as I was passing him he said, ' Captain, don't leave me here.' I said I would not. After getting my company secure, I called for some one to help me bring Lieut. Newcomb off the field; but knowing how warm a place we had been in, no one except First Sergeant Wallace T. George dared to risk his safety. We went to him amid a shower of bullets, and he said, when we undertook to lift him, ' Don't touch my legs.' So we took him by the arms, dragging his legs the while, got him through the fence, laid him on the ground, then put him on a stretcher, and sent him to the Lacy House Hospital, across the river, where he died. He said toward the last, ' It's all light ahead!' "

General Luther Stephenson, Jr., has kindly allowed the use of one of his photographs in preparing the cut of the Lacy House here presented.

Col. Chadwick and others recall the seemingly prophetic remark of Newcomb, previous to the battle of Fredericksburg, that " he did not expect to come out of another battle safely."

Colonel Devereux also bears testimony to Newcomb's self-sacrificing spirit: " His regiment being ordered to charge the batteries directly in front, there were shot down in the storm of bullets that met them no less than eight color-bearers in succession. At one time both were killed at once, and both colors lay on the ground. Here was an opportunity for a self-sacrificing manhood that young Newcomb was eminently fitted to put forth. Rushing to the front he seized both colors and waved his regiment on. But the inevitable consequences followed. Like all who had preceded him, and those that followed, every man that bore the colors was the fated object of the unerring bullets of the enemy's sharpshooters whilst the regiment remained in the open field. Newcomb was wounded in both legs, which were very much shattered."

"We were at the front," writes Captain J. G. B. Adams, Postmaster of Lynn, Mass., "when our regiment and the 7th Michigan led the 'Forlorn Hope' and crossed the river in boats under a terrible fire from the Rebels on the other shore. We fought together in the streets of Fredericksburg, and on the 13th of December charged Marye's Heights with the regiment. We must force our regiment over the Heights. Never was such a terrific fire concentrated upon any body of men as was on us that day. We advanced with the Colors, and the Sergeants fell dead at our feet. A Corporal grasps the flag before it strikes the ground, and he in turn goes down. Newcomb catches the flag as he falls; the Sergeant with the State flag is killed; Newcomb grasps that also, and is shot through both legs. Handing the flags to me he said, 'John, don't let them go down.' And with the flags in my hands, we charged across the field and secured the advance of the regiment. I was promoted for it, but poor Newcomb gave his life to save the flag. I saw him for a moment that night, only to tell him that the boys did not fail us, and that the flag was safe. You may think that I mention *myself* in this more than is proper; but I cannot tell the story of Lieut. Newcomb without telling my own, as our war record was the same while he lived. I could tell this story much better than I can write it. My eyes fill with tears and my hand trembles, as I recall those days and think of the noble fellows who went down in the fight. Braver men never followed the flag than were found in the ranks of the 19th Reg't. We left nearly half of the men engaged that day. We could not have carried Marye's Heights if we had fought until this time, but good soldiers do not question orders.

'Theirs not to make reply,
Theirs but to do and die.'

So we did our best. I was in command of Co. I that day."
First Sergeant Wallace T. George, (afterward First Lieut.

in the 37th U. S. C. Infantry) and now Street Commissioner of Haverhill, Mass., writes as follows: "Upon the battle field at Fredericksburg, at Capt. J. C. Chadwick's request, I went to the assistance of Lieut. Newcomb, and asked him if both of his legs were broken. He answered, 'Only one.' Then I asked, 'Can you endure it to be taken by the arms?' He replied, 'I can bear anything; only get me off this field.'"

Captain W. E. Barrows, now President of the Williamantic Linen Co., Conn., furnishes further information of great value. He went out with the 19th as Hospital Steward, and served in that capacity at the battle of Fredericksburg. "It was my good fortune," he writes, "to hear soon after his (Newcomb's) wound of his condition, and I visited him in the Lacy House. Mortally wounded as he was, he found strength to speak to me of a better world, and a glorious future for those that stand fast to the end· My duties at that terrible time did not allow me to stay with him as long as I wished; but his conduct and admonition to me made an impression never to be forgotten, and it must have made me a better man."

The Surgeon and Assistant Surgeon of the regiment died a few years ago, and we lose the testimony which they doubtless would have been glad to furnish. In fourteen battles and skirmishes previous to the action at Fredericksburg, Lieut. Newcomb was providentially preserved, and his first wounds were those received on Dec. 13, 1862. Colonel John C. Chadwick writes: "I don't know as I can give you the names of all the battles, but I will try. First there was Ball's Bluff (Edward's Ferry); then Lee's Mills, Yorktown, West Point, Fair Oaks, Fair Oaks (June 25th), Peach Orchard, Savage Station, White Oak Swamp, Glendale, Malvern Hill, Malvern Hill (2d time), Antietam, and Fredericksburg. By referring to a memorandum which I had saved, I am able to give them to you in the order in which they came."

Captain Stephen J. Newman writes: "During the battle called 'Ball's Bluff,' two companies of the 19th (H and K) under Major H. J. How crossed at Edward's Ferry to Virginia, and skirmished all day with the enemy. It is there that Corporals

Newcomb and Manning were with Brig. Gen. Fred. Lander when Lander received his death wound. The Regimental Color has on it 'Edward's Ferry.'

You ask for other places that the regiment was engaged in, to the time of my discharge, viz:

April 8, '62. Yorktown, reconnoissance and skirmish,—and under a siege fire till the evacuation of the same, May 2d, '62.

May 7, '62. Battle of West Point, Va., not much.

May 31, June 1, '62. Battle of Fair Oaks,—only as re-enforcements, not in the action.

June 26, '62. Fair Oak Swamp. This was the first tough fight of the regiment.

June 29, '62. Battles of Peach Orchard and Savage Station, all day. I was left at Peach Orchard.

June 30, '62. Battle of White Oak Swamp. Battle of Nelson's Farm. This was a very hard fight.

July 17, '62. Second Malvern Hill, reconnoissance two days.

Sept. 6, '62. Battle or skirmish of Fairfax Court House. We were the rear-guard of that portion of the army.

Sept. 14, '62. South Mountain, Md. Arrived during the night to commence on the 15th, but did not participate. Rebs evacuated during the night.

Sept. 16, '62. Boonesboro', Md. Re-enforced the skirmishers— no fight.

Sept. 17, '62. Battle of Antietam, Md. This was a hot one.

Oct. 2, '62. Halltown, Va. Skirmish.''

A few additional particulars concerning the battle of Fredericksburg must suffice. "Officers of the 19th Regiment relate that they saw an officer on horseback, waving his sword. A shell came and took his head off smooth, but the headless officer still rode along for some distance, the hand waving his sword, proving the strength of the ruling passion in death." The Regimental report after the battle was as follows: "Officers killed, 1; officers wounded, 8; enlisted men killed, 13; enlisted men wounded, 75; enlisted men missing, 7." Major (then Captain) H. G. O. Weymouth was very seriously wounded while gallantly leading the regiment. Telegrams to Boston papers contained the following: Lieut. E. M. Newcomb of Co. C, wounded in both legs, mortally." "Lieut. Newcomb who had both legs shot, cannot recover, and will not probably be living when this reaches the *Herald*."

It will be remembered that on the morning of Dec. 13 Lieut. Newcomb, knowing that a fearful battle was impending, endeavored to insure the safety of his younger brother by sending him after a box which had been left at Potomac Creek, a few miles from the front. Soon after Charlie's departure the battle commenced. Hearing the heavy firing he hastened to the telegraph station at Potomac Creek, and learned that the 19th Mass. was engaged. With great anxiety he awaited the departure of of the next train at 2 P. M. After a short passage he arrived at Falmouth, deposited the box in a place of safety, and started for the battle field. Wearing a soldier's overcoat he was not challenged at the pontoon bridge. Crossing the Rappahannock he spent the afternoon just in the rear of the line of battle. He retains a vivid recollection of the scene, and thus describes it. "Regiment after regiment of the reserves was ordered to the front, and marched forward with cheers. I saw the 22d Mass.— fragments of it—return. Shot and shell fell into the churches we used as hospitals. In charging the rifle-pits near the stone wall, Edgar fell. I passed through the entire length of the city, re-crossed the river on the lower pontoon about sunset, and made my way to the Lacy House. As I was passing in, I met some one who said my brother was wounded. I found him lying on the floor, and conscious. On recovering from shock the next morning, his first thought was in regard to his sword, which had been left behind. On Sunday afternoon, Dec. 14, at Edgar's urgent request I went across the river to find the sword. It had been unbuckled when he was placed on the stretcher. I found his regiment in the city, and came up with them as they were mustered for roll call. You can perhaps imagine something of that roll call after the battle. More than half their brave fellows had been left upon the field.

I recovered the sword which his men had guarded jealously, and which they said they would have brought away at any cost. It was my brother's legacy to me, and I value it above all other possessions."

It would be painful to surviving friends to dwell at length upon the week of torture in the hospital. A few words will suffice. After examining the wounds the surgeons very properly declined to operate. They were uncertain whether the injuries were caused by a bullet or a fragment of shell. During those long days of agony, Charlie was a faithful nurse in constant attendance. Colonel Chadwick and others assisted as far as they were able. Several army-friends visited Edgar, and he conversed calmly and cheerfully of the future, while not an eye was dry but his. Kind messages were sent to friends at home. The Bible which had been so often read in camp was bequeathed to his only sister. "Tell mother," he said, "that I shall be near her; perhaps nearer than ever before. Perhaps I can help her more. Precious little mother."

"His brother," writes the Rev. J. C. Fernald, "could hear him softly repeating, 'Perfect through suffering—perfect through suffering.' He held and watched wistfully the pictured faces of those dear ones he was to see no more on earth; and in an interval of comparative freedom from pain he sent to each a special message. He gave directions that no words of praise be placed upon his tombstone."

When Charlie shed tears at the approaching separation, Edgar said, "Your orders are not yet come. When they come, you will join me if you live well." With perfect coolness he made preparations for death, selecting a most appropriate text for his funeral sermon. The welcome release from suffering came on the morning of Saturday, December 20, before dawn. At the closing scene in that little room, Charlie, a soldier, and Miss Clara Barton [now President of the American Red Cross Association] were present. Charlie read the seventeenth chapter of St. John's Gospel, and Edgar repeated it. Toward the last his mind was wandering, and he imagined that the nurse, Miss Barton, was his mother. She kindly favored the illusion by shading the light. Charlie and Miss Barton, at Edgar's request, made an effort to sing a hymn or two—"The Shining Shore," "For O we stand, on Jordan's strand," &c. His father, Mr. John J. Newcomb, arrived on the following morning, Sunday, Dec. 21.

Edgar's body was then in the embalmer's tent. The remains arrived at Mr. Newcomb's residence in Boston on Christmas evening.

The Boston Journal published an obituary as follows:

"We are pained to announce the decease of Lieut. Edgar M. Newcomb of the 19th Mass. Regiment. He died at Falmouth, Va., from the effects of the wounds he received during the battle of Fredericksburg. He was in full possession of all his faculties, and peacefully fell asleep, in the full faith of Christian hope, to wake no more in this life. A younger brother was with him to soothe his dying hours by the kind offices of affection. His father had started for Falmouth, but did not arrive in season to see him before he died.

Thus another brave and cherished son of Massachusetts has laid his life a noble sacrifice upon his country's altar. Lieut. Newcomb was a young man of fine character and education, a true Christian, and controlled by the most patriotic impulses. He graduated from Harvard College in the Class of 1860, and had entered upon the active pursuits of life when the war broke out. With a generous disregard of his pecuniary interests, and the attractions of a home surrounded by all that makes life pleasing, he volunteered as a soldier in the ranks, to defend the government of his fathers, and assert its rightful supremacy. By his capacity, bravery and firmness, he won the respect and confidence of his superiors, and was advanced to the post of Lieutenant. He was a true man, an unselfish patriot, and a brave soldier. A numerous circle of relatives and friends will lament his untimely decease. He was about twenty-two years of age, just in the flower of youth."

Other extracts are taken from the same paper:

"The members of the Harvard Class of 1860, now in this city, met yesterday to take appropriate notice of the death of Lieut. E. M. Newcomb, who fell at Fredericksburg in the recent battle. Resolutions were passed testifying their respect for his character, his Christian humility and faithfulness to duty, his courage and death from honorable wounds on the field of battle, and expressive of sympathy with his family."

"At a meeting of the Boston Corn Exchange this morning, of which the father of Lieut. Newcomb is a member, appropriate notice was taken of the death of Lieut. Newcomb, and it was voted to adjourn for the purpose of attending the funeral."

At noon on Saturday, Dec. 27, 1862, the public obsequies

took place, as will be seen from the following account taken from the Boston Journal:

FUNERAL OF LIEUT. NEWCOMB.

" Man goeth to his long home, and the mourners go about the streets."
Ecclesiastes XII. 5.

"The last sad offices which the living can perform for the dead were to-day rendered to the remains of Lieut. Edgar M. Newcomb of the Massachusetts 19th Regiment, who received mortal wounds at the battle of Fredericksburg, and died on the 20th instant at Falmouth, Va. The funeral services took place at 12 o'clock, in Park-street church, of which religious society the deceased was a member. The sanctuary where he had been accustomed to join in the worship of God was filled with his numerous friends and the general public, come to pay their sad tribute of respect to one who had lived and died like a Christian—who amid the license of camp life had exhibited the noblest traits of genuine piety—who had bravely stood ' in the fore front of battle ' on many a hard fought field —and who, when confronted by the King of Terrors, calmly, peacefully, gladly welcomed the hour when the mortal should put on immortality, and death be swallowed up in victory.

Among the prominent individuals present were Governor Andrew, Senator Wilson, Colonel Hinks, Major Rice and Captain Rice of the 19th Regiment, together with a large body of military men and college classmates. The casket was deposited in front of the altar, wrapped in the folds of the American flag, and covered with wreaths of immortelles and fragrant flowers. The military cap, pierced with bullets, and sword of the gallant soldier, bearing similiar marks, were also placed upon the casket, which bore the inscription:

EDGAR M. NEWCOMB,
LIEUT. 19TH REGIMENT, MASS. VOLS.,
DIED DEC. 20TH, 1862,
AT FALMOUTH, VA.,
OF WOUNDS RECEIVED AT THE BATTLE OF FREDERICKSBURG.
AGED 22 YEARS, 2 MONTHS, 18 DAYS.

In front of the altar were arranged the tattered ensigns of the 19th Regiment, which were at the battle of Antietam, and which spoke volumes of the heroic deeds and unflinching courage of the glorious 19th, of which the deceased was no small part.

The services opened with singing, [by a quartette] followed by prayer and the reading of select passages of Scripture by Rev. Mr. Todd. The choir then sang the beautiful hymn commencing, ' I would not live alway.' Rev. J. O. Means, D. D., of Roxbury, then delivered a beautiful and affectionate tribute to the memory of the deceased.

The sermon is given below:—

Our young friend, as he was falling asleep, expressed the wish that one who loved him well, would preach a sermon over his remains, from the text: "Until the day break, and the shadows flee away." The words are in the 2nd Chapter of Solomon's Song, and 17th verse. "Until the day break, and the shadows flee away." Precious, pregnant sentence; telling whither his longing eyes were gazing, telling where our strength and consolation may be found.

Until the day break, we cannot comprehend the strange events which are now transpiring. It is too dark yet; our eyes are filled with tears; we cannot compose our thoughts to judge the mysterious tribulations of our country, and the deep anguish of sorrowing hearts, as we shall judge them when all the shadows shall flee away, and the fulness of the coming day break forth.

If we go into one of our workshops, we see the forge glowing and flashing, as the bars of iron are thrust in among the coals; we hear the ringing strokes by which the tough metal is beaten into shape. Flanges of enormous screws and ribs not set up, are lying around, and sections of keel, and segments of boilers; huge beams are slowly sliding under the hammers, and armor plates curved by the maul under heat and pressure are bolted together; there is no symmetry apparent, but utter confusion and disorder, and the noises do not resemble the music of the spheres. Until the work is completed, and the iron ship is launched, the monster guns are mounted in the turret, and the grim monitor is ready for service, we cannot understand the movements of the workshop.

And when men's lives fall upon the period when God is giving new shape to the institutions of society, building a monitor impregnable to the bolts of wrong, while the changes are in progress, the dust and heat and turmoil which accompany the process, occupy our thoughts. It is what we are suffering, it is the pressure that is upon us, the terrible sacrifices, the heavy blows that fall in quick succession; it is the anxiety that clouds the future, which we dwell upon. And what it all means, and how to look upon these scenes, we shall not understand, until the day breaks. When this sublime work is completed, when the wise Providence of God has brought about the changes which He is working, as the glory of the new day shines across the continent, it will illuminate these gloomy battle-fields; and oh! it will fall upon the faces of our martyred dead, so that when we look upon them, it will seem as if we " saw the face of an angel."

The clear, spiritual discernment of this young soldier, recognized the danger that we should sit down in the gloom and sorrow of this hour, and while the sackcloth is upon us, and ashes cover our heads, should mourn and lament, and say, Alas, all this sacrifice, this profusion of treasure spent, and of blood; to what purpose is this waste? How much might our noble boys have done for their country and for God? How much might their lives have contributed towards the happiness of loving hearts; towards elevating the nation in all earthly prosperities? What were they not worth, to become heralds of salvation, and to bring this sinful world back to God and heaven? And now, the alabaster box is broken, the precious life is poured out, and nothing gained.

Hark! out of those lips which we hoped to hear speak some day from this pulpit, there come in gentle, peaceful breathing, the words, " Until the day break "—not now—judge not our work, judge not our country's crisis, ask not what it means, do not question yet the wisdom of that which the loving kindness of God is arranging; wait till the shadows flee away.

We must transport ourselves into the future, and look upon the gloom of these days of rebellion, as it will appear from the height to which God, through all this discipline, is lifting this nation. Valley Forge does not look now as it did in 1778. Not one drop too much of blood was spilt, not one pang too sharp was endured, not one sacrifice too great was made for what the daybreak has revealed, and what two generations have rejoiced in. And when the present struggle shall be over, and it takes its place among the sternest and sublimest convulsions by which the powers of darkness have ever tried to overthrow or hinder the establishment of the kingdom of righteousness and peace, the costly offerings which praying fathers and mothers have laid upon the altar, the setting up the walls in the blood of the first-born and fairest of our sons, all that has been done and suffered in the awful baptism of fire through which we are passing, it will not seem then to have been too much.

If we cannot lift ourselves out of our calamity, to judge rightly of these events, and if we cannot wait for the daybreak; nay, if we doubt whether there is to be any daybreak, and say in our despair that the spheres have done revolving, and the sun has been taken down from the heavens, and the universe given over to darkness and eternal eclipse; if it seems to us that God has forgotten to be gracious, and in wrath will not remember mercy, but will give us up to utter desolation, so that the shadows shall never flee away; then let me say that there is comfort in the thought, that these brave men have gone up where they stand nearer the Throne, and know better the purposes of Infinite Justice, and discern with a clearer and more radiant vision what is to be unrolled out of the dark future.

To him, and to such as he,—the noble army of martyrs, whose coronation days we are celebrating—to him, the day has broken; and what daylight it is that fills those eyelids!

> "Bright on the holy mountain round the throne,
> Bright, where in borrowed light, the far stars shone,
> Regions on regions, far away they shine.
> 'Tis light ineffable—'tis light divine!
> Immortal light, and life forever more!"

We are left in no uncertainty. We know that before his eager vision the shadows have fled away. His dying words were: "'Tis all light ahead." He need not have spoken thus, to assure us, for it is all light behind. The radiance which now encompasses him is not so strange, for it flows back over his earthly life. In the brief period of twenty-two years which rounded his life last October, not many eventful scenes have transpired; and it is the tersest encomium upon the happiness of his life, that is marked by little of that *falling out*, which is the meaning of *event*.

Born in Troy, New York, October 2d, 1840; his parents removed to this city, when he was a few months old, and he received Christian baptism, by the name of Edgar Marshall, in the Central Church, Winter Street. His life has been in Boston. He received his education in the Grammar and Latin Schools, from which last he passed in due order to Harvard College, and graduated in 1860. He is in the fullest and best sense a child of this city; and may God bless the city and the Commonwealth which breeds such sons!

It had long been his joyful purpose to become a minister of the gospel; but his health broke down before the close of his college course, and without remaining till Commencement, he went abroad in the summer of 1860, and spent the autumn in travelling on foot through England and France, with the hope of regaining health. Not wholly succeeding, on returning he entered his father's counting house and engaged in active business for a while. The breaking out of the rebellion found him in this position. From the endearments of the happiest of homes he did not hesitate a moment to tear himself away. Proposing to offer his whole life to his master in heaven, he came forward to do his bidding first as a private soldier in the great army of freedom. He enlisted in the ranks of the 19th Regiment, when it was first formed and unknown to fame, and has shared its fortunes and contributed to its glory, in all the great achievements which make it so illustrious. Earning his promotion, step by step, he became Sergeant Major, and Second and finally, First Lieutenant, "And I never expect to go higher," he wrote home. Was it a presentiment that he was going so soon to the highest?

When that gloriously tattered ensign of the old 19th, which looks as though it had been stripped, thread by thread, to bind up the wounds of the gallant men who have carried it aloft, and followed it where the bullets whizzed loudest; when what there is left of battered staff and bent spear-head, and clotted ribbons, is held out by the historian, who shall come to make up the bead roll of the heroic sons of Massachusetts, among all the gallant dead, whose names will be blazoned on the escutcheon, that of Lieut. Newcomb will not stand in the lowest place. He was a soldier, like so many whom Massachusetts has sent, against all the impulses of a tender and beautiful nature, in crucifixion of his peaceful and loving spirit, from the simple and strong impulses of christian duty. Putting aside his repugnance to that which might be deemed hardening in the life of camps, not knowing what the vindictive and belligerent quarrelsomeness of the born fighter is, a man of womanly purity and refinement, blushing at the suggestion of anything that would pollute his virtue, as quickly as at anything that would stain his honor; with an instinctive and irrepressible sense of what right demanded, and with a conscientious and eager readiness to do her behests, he sprang forward with alacrity, as a child of his country, and of his God. He felt that the interest of both was involved, and that both alike bade him go. And oh! how many of these noblest of soldiers, specimen men, have gone where he has gone—onward and upward!

It was a great change, to take musket and knapsack, for one whose life and love had been where his had been. His tastes were for books, he had a poetic temperament, which found delight in music; he was of a delicate, sensitive, self-contained nature, not readily making acquaintances; of singular modesty, genial and communicative with those who liked inward thoughts, studying deeply the mysteries of the soul, and revolving the great questions of life and destiny. His face had not lost the red and white tints of beautiful boyhood when he went away, and the long, pensive eye-lashes hid a full, liquid, hazel eye. And his mind and heart were as unstained as his person.

I have spoken of these things, because many overlook how such qualities knit into the most enduring, most manly, and most soldierly character. Instead of drawing back from the great privations which our noble troops have endured, he has never been wont to speak of them. We knew that there were great hardships, but his letters did not hint at it, save when his playful fancy was painting a humorous picture for his friends. He sometimes spoke of the hardships of the poor fellows around him; but he never grumbled about his own fare or condition; and, in fact, this patient, cheerful endurance kept him not only in health, but built up his youthful person into the stalwart, sinewy, muscular frame of an athletic man.

I am not the one to speak of him as a soldier, you who led him on, and you who fought by his side will do that. * * *

How it plants him forever in the hearts of men of Massachusetts, to know that he received his death wound holding aloft *her* colors!

The glory of your regiment was all the glory he desired. It is beautiful to see how devotion to his colors sometimes pushes aside the extreme modesty which never tells his friends of anything which he has done, and compels him to speak of the regiment and what the great General thinks of it. * * *

Through the fourteen battles and skirmishes of this heroic regiment, he had passed unscathed, and in the desperate, forlorn hope of memorable crossing. But in the fierce attacks of Saturday, cheering on the men, waving the flag, with bullets through his hat and blanket, and coat, and canteen, one tore through both legs, and brought him down; and after enduring excruciating pain till Saturday morning of the ensuing week,

"God's finger touched him and he slept."

The foundation, not simply of his soldierly virtues, but of his whole beautiful manly character, was a strong, inwrought faith in the Lord Jesus Christ. At the age of eleven years he became a Christian, and he entered the full communion of the church in the place where his dear body now reposes, when he was fourteen. And from his spiritual birthday until the last farewell to the men of his company, as one by one they came to his cot, last week Friday, and received his dying message to meet him in heaven, his piety has been growing brighter and brighter to the perfect day. With great breadth and depth of intelligent principle, there was a perennial out-gushing of his religious feelings. His christian character was developed with unusual symmetry, the solemnity of the great things being balanced by a winning cheerfulness and joyousness. I think his religious life took no harm from all the temptations of the camp. Since he has gone, what we had not known has come to our knowledge, that he frequently preached, and held prayer meetings in camp, and performed such religious services, that some of the pious chaplains supposed he belonged to their number. When his time had come, Christ was all in all to him. To his brother officers, his fellow soldiers and friends, he earnestly commended his and their Redeemer. "It never seemed before to me, so great and noble a thing to die. I had hoped to preach the gospel, but I shall serve my country better in heaven."

Yes! Will not the example of such a noble Christian and soldier, translated to heaven, do for the country what his sword and pen could not do, if he had lived? * * *

With messages to all he loved, distributing his remembrances, asking that no words of praise be placed on his tombstone, but simply, "Lieutenant Edgar M. Newcomb, of the 19th Mass:" this young soldier, his life protracted with torture, with home and heaven rising before his vision, had his last thoughts on christian charities, and away there in sound of battle, devised his property equally to the Societies for Home and for Foreign Missions.

His last letter was written Saturday morning, and was in his pocket when he fell, and was taken out and forwarded. And the last sentence he wrote is: "C. thinks I owe my past safety to the prayers of my friends; I have often thought the same, and when I consider the temptations of this most trying life, my protection from sin is more marvelous than from wounds and death. Good bye."

Until the day break and the shadows flee away!

> "How calm and blest,
>   The dead now rest,
> Who in the Lord departed;
> All their works do follow them,
>   Yea, they sleep glad-hearted.
>   Oh! Blessed Rock!
>   Soon grant Thy flock
> To see Thy Sabbath morning!
> Strife and pain will all be past
>   When that day is dawning."

When I had written thus, I learned that in asking that I would preach on this text, he added: "Let it be applied to the country and to myself." So, unconscious of his wishes, I had applied it For him, to you whose heads are bowed in sorrow, what words could come so full of comfort. Put this verse back into the chapter where he found it, and see what his happy soul was saying to you. The third verse of the chapter reads:

" I sat down under the shadow of my beloved with great delight, and his fruit was sweet to my taste, and his banner over me was love. His left hand is under my head, and his right hand doth embrace me."

It was not his younger, it was his Elder Brother who held his dying head!

" My beloved is mine and I am his. He feedeth among the lillies: until the day break, and the shadows flee away." How near that is. How near to us the daybreak which shall herald us into the companionship of those who have gone before,—the glorious daybreak for us also! There is nothing possible to mourn over, save that such a life ended so suddenly. But how full the life was, how long, over-passing the life of men who exist doing nothing, or doing wrong, till three score and ten. He has done more than any of us, for he has done what God appointed him to do, and finished and reached home before the sun had climbed the zenith.

Classmates and friends! and all who have led him and stood with him by that battle-rent ensign! Companions in arms, and ye who have come from the high seats of Magistracy, glad to do meet honor to this young citizen who had but just come of age, but whose heroic life has made the red blood mantle the checks of the oldest with pride: he gave himself, first to God, and then and thus to his country. Can any of you do better? Will you do as well!

Father, mother, sister, brother,—Until the day break!

After the exercise in the church, many of the congregation availed themselves of an opportunity to view the remains. The long funeral procession then slowly moved to Mount Auburn Cemetery,—a sacred enclosure where, during his college course, Edgar had spent many pleasant and profitable hours with friends who still mourn his loss. The pall-bearers were Captain Chamberlain, of the First Regiment, Mass. Vols.; Captain Hovey, of the 13th Regiment; Captain Carey, of the 13th Regiment; Captain Kent, of the 23d Regiment; Lieutenant Russell, of the 12th Regiment; Lieutenant Trull, of the 5th Battery. It was near sunset on that sad wintry day, when those who were nearest in kinship and friendship looked for the last time upon the pale but still beautiful face. The remains were deposited in the family lot on Sedge Path, and we returned home with desolate hearts which were only relieved by looking forward to the promised daybreak.

After more than twenty years, some of us are still waiting amid the shadows of earth; solaced by the precious hope that, in the good time appointed by our heavenly Father, the shadows will forever flee away.

Lines composed in honor of Chaplain Fuller of the 16th Massachusetts are equally applicable to Lieut. Newcomb.

> " Servant of God, thy race is run,
> Life's toils and trials o'er ;
> A crown of glory thou has won,
> By Rappahannock's shore."

A faithful drawing of Edgar's monument at Mount Auburn is represented on this page.

> " And yet I trust that all who weep,
> Somewhere, at last, will surely find
> His rest, if through dark ways they keep
> The child-like faith, the prayerful mind ;
> And some far Christmas morn shall bring
> From human ills a sweet release
> To loving hearts, while angels sing,—
> ' Peace and good will, good will and peace !' "

At Park-street church, Boston, on either side of the pulpit, are memorial tablets, bearing in red letters the names of deceased soldiers who formerly belonged to the society. The first inscription on one of the tablets is as follows:

LIEUT. EDGAR M. NEWCOMB,
19TH MASS. VOL. REG'T,
WOUNDED AT THE BATTLE OF FREDERICKSBURG, VA., DEC. 13,
DIED AT FALMOUTH, VA., DEC. 20, 1862, AGED 22 YEARS.

Above and below the tablet are other appropriate inscriptions:

I. H. S.
IN MEMORIAM.
DULCE ET DECORUM EST PRO PATRIA MORI.

Near the entrance of the new Latin School building in Boston "stands a statue by Richard S. Greenough, a Latin School boy, which was erected by the graduates of the school to honor those who had honored her, and to commemorate those who had fallen in defending their country. This statue represents the *alma mater* of the school resting on a shield which bears the names of the dead, and extending a laurel crown to reward those who returned." The name of Lieut. Newcomb occupies a prominent position on the shield. His portrait may be seen in the exhibition hall of the Latin School.

Harvard University has not forgotten to honor her noble sons who gave their lives in defence of the Union. The impressive architectural beauty of Memorial Hall attracts the attention of every visitor. A solemn stillness pervades the transept containing the white marble tablets in memory of departed heroes. The fallen patriots of the class of 1860 are immortalized on several of these tablets. At the top of one of them is this inscription:

EDGAR MARSHALL NEWCOMB,
20 DECEMBER, 1862, FREDERICKSBURG.

A more touching memorial may still be seen at Falmouth, Va. During the week of Edgar's intense agony at the Lacy House Hospital, a profuse hemorrhage took place, and a large pool of blood stained the floor. About fifteen years after the battle, Mr. Charles B. Newcomb again visited the Lacy House. Receiving permission to inspect the premises, he went directly to the room where his brother died, and once more gazed upon the indelible blood-stain. Early in the present year, in reply to a note of inquiry, the following courteous letter was received:

CHATHAM, STAFFORD CO., VA.
JAN. 9, 1883.

DEAR SIR:—

Your letter addressed to Major J. Horace Lacy was handed me by that gentleman to reply, as my father occupies Chatham House, or Lacy House as it was called during the war. It was built by a lawyer, Wm. Henry Fitz Hugh, of London. The style of the building is exactly the same as that of Lord Chatham's in Stafford-shire, England. Therefore it derived its name, Chatham. The House has a romantic history, in which George Washington, Thomas Jefferson, LaFayette, Randolph and others figured conspicuously.

I remember distinctly the occasion of Mr. Charles Newcomb's visit to our house about five years ago. He seemed to be familiar with the location of the room where his brother died. He went straight to it without being shown. It was an affecting scene to see him kneeling over his brother's blood, which still remains on the floor, and can never be erased.

Yours very truly,
H. WATSON SHADLE.

George Washington and his widowed mother resided for a short time on Stafford Heights, near the site of the Lacy House, and afterwards in the city of Fredericksburg.

The following additional tributes to Newcomb's excellent qualities have been cheerfully contributed by his companions in arms. They had abundant opportunity to form a correct estimate of his character, having associated with him constantly during the last fifteen months of his life, and under most trying circumstances.

From Col. Devereux: "As an officer, he was prompt, careful and zealous, kind to his men, but a good disciplinarian."

From Col. Chadwick: "Newcomb was respected by officers and men, and many times since the war have I heard him spoken very highly and kindly of. He was thoroughly brave, but yet realized the danger he went into."

From Capt. William A. Hill: "While I knew Edgar M. Newcomb and respected his many noble qualities, I have often felt that I knew him better dead than living. I can perhaps make myself better understood in this connection, if I say that, although in years we were about equal, yet in maturity of thought and judgment he was the superior of us all; and it is now through the clearer vision of matured judgment that we see plainly and esteem more highly his virtues; and I have often told to my boy the story of his life as I knew it; of the heroic devotion to the cause in which we felt a common interest, of the quiet and unassuming manner which characterized his every act, of the gentlemanly and dignified bearing at all times, of the consistent christian life which he led, when the test was always the severest, and of that last gallant act of his life, when in the thickest of that terrible battle of Fredericksburg, when both colors went down in the hands of their wounded bearers, Newcomb sprang and seized them, and with one in each hand went bravely forward to receive the death wounds which followed so swiftly his noble act.

To a person of his extremely refined tastes the associations of camp life must have been anything but attractive. He enlisted as a private soldier, not because he was carried away by the excitement of the times, not because he longed for glory and fame, not because he felt himself fitted for such a life of hardship, exposure and danger; but he was found in the front rank with his face always to the enemy, because he firmly and conscientiously believed it to be his duty to do his part in the great struggle for the maintenance of our National Union. From my knowledge of the man I know that he faced the dread messenger even as he faced the trials and dangers of his soldier life, with a quiet, calm composure, and with brave though meek submission to the will of his Father. I have alluded to the fact of his having been a thoroughly consistent, conscientious christian, and would support that statement by saying that he made it a rule to read a chapter in his Bible every night on retiring."

From Capt. J. G. B. Adams: "You cannot write in too high praise of the bravery of Lieut. Newcomb. With no taste for army life he entered the army because duty called him, and he died the death of the true loyal soldier."

From Capt. Stephen J. Newman: "I regarded Lieut. Newcomb as a brave patriot and a true christian soldier. Edgar used to read his Bible and pray when others were asleep. In fact he was a refined christian and a quiet gentleman, and had none of that which is known as religious gush. I liked him for his excellent manly qualities. He was a man of excellent parts."

From Capt. J. P. Reynolds: "Newcomb was a good official, most faithful in the discharge of his duties (which he had an unusually conscientious perception of) and entirely free from the rollicking disposition which characterizes so many in army life. He certainly was an exemplary young man, visiting the hospital and ministering to the physical wants of the sick, and officiating with the Chaplain in ministering to the spiritual wants of both the sick and well, upon his own responsibility, when off duty. He always had a wonderful regard for the wishes and feelings of others, regardless of himself—another trait so often wanting in life in the service."

From Capt. James H. Rice: I know he was a brave, conscientious, christian soldier, a thorough gentleman, consistent in everything."

From Capt. W. F. Rice (now Q. M., 23d U. S. Infantry, at Fort Union, New Mexico): "He was a thorough christian in every respect, and a man for whom I think all who knew him had the highest regard."

From Capt. (formerly Hospital Steward) W. E. Barrows: "He was a gentleman, a conscientious christian soldier, a bright and shining light in the regiment. In any community where an honest and upright life is esteemed, he would have been a marked man. But in the army, where temptations to let go some of the finer points of a christian life are great, and where it was sometimes difficult with most men to find communion with the Heavenly Father, it never seemed so with him. Like all the precious metals, the more he was rubbed the brighter he would shine. * * After he was wounded I took all the care, personally, I could find time to do."

From Lieut. Wallace T. George: "I gladly give my testimony to the integrity and uprightness of Lieut. Newcomb's character, and his manly independence and personal courage."

From Sergeant C. R. Hazen: "I can say with all sincerity that every one who knew Mr. Newcomb, knew his character to be of the sterling sort. His principle was strict integrity, and his devotion to religious duty was very remarkable. Nothing but circumstances entirely beyond his control could have the slightest influence in turning him from a strict performance of that duty. Every day he read his Bible, however arduous his military duties might be (and a soldier's duties in active service are not mere child's play.) Many times I have seen him sit down in his tent for that purpose. He would perhaps read a verse or two before being observed by his companions, but the discovery would be no sooner made than he would be greeted with jeers, or made the butt of some joke. The poor boy would close his book and leave the tent, without a word of remonstrance, and seek some more retired spot and resume his reading. I never heard him utter one harsh, hasty word. All was borne with quiet patience."

From Charles A. Newhall, clerk of the Regimental Association: " I remember Lieut. Newcomb perfectly well as a good soldier and a sincere christian,—one who was always ready for duty, and who always had a kind word for every one." Dr J. W. Sawyer and several other members of the 19th Mass. have sent similar letters, praising Lieut. Newcomb in terms of the highest respect and admiration.

It has been stated that Governor Andrew was present at the funeral. Shortly after, in his address to the Legislature, His Excellency used the following language, evidently suggested by the discourse of Dr. Means: "The flag, whose standard-bearer, shot down in battle, tossed it from his dying hand, nerved by undying patriotism, has been caught by a comrade, who in turn has closed his eyes for the last time upon its starry folds, as another hero-martyr clasped the splintered staff, and rescued the symbol at once of country and of blood-bought fame. How can the fleeting words of human praise gild the record of their glory? From the din of battle they have passed to the peace of eternity." At the funeral of Lieut. Col. George E. Marshall, Gov. Bullock delivered an eloquent and touching address, from which a short paragraph is taken: " All generations shall commemorate their valor and their patriotism. No ties of kindred can impose limitations upon the grief and gratitude in which they shall be held and treasured. The country shall be their monument."

In the Book of Job are these words: " With clouds He covereth the light; and commandeth it not to shine by the cloud that cometh betwixt. * * And now men see not the bright light which is in the clouds: but the wind passeth, and cleanseth them." Already the shadows are beginning to " flee away," and in some degree we can understand why " that dark night of national disaster " was permitted at Fredericksburg. A complete and decisive Union victory might have led to premature negotiations for peace. Such action would probably have rendered inoperative the preliminary Proclamation of Emancipation. Gen. Lee was victorious, all the Southern States were waging war against the Federal Government on January 1, 1863, and the fate of slavery was sealed. Thus the untold suffering at Fredericksburg contributed not a little toward securing the inevitable and speedy abolition of slavery.

> " They never fail
> Who die in a great cause."

"They that die for a good cause are redeemed from death. Their names are gathered and garnered. Their memory is precious."

Our little sketch is hastening to a close; not because there is nothing more to be said, but simply because space is limited. There is an eternity before us, where the record of faithful service will be open for inspection. Henceforth, let us think of our hero as one of the glorified saints of that Better Land; in which "THERE SHALL BE NO MORE DEATH, NEITHER SORROW, NOR CRYING, NEITHER SHALL THERE BE ANY MORE PAIN: FOR THE FORMER THINGS ARE PASSED AWAY."